DEVIANCE

BOOK 7

SYLVIA WILCOX MYSTERIES

BRAYLEE PARKINSON

PROLOGUE

Bruce Carpenter had deliberately chosen the last shift of the day at Bayou Sauvage. New Year's Eve always spurred a party atmosphere in the city, and the late shift was—as he'd expected—almost free of visitors. His drive to New Orleans East had been uneventful, with traffic moving at normal speeds. Since the visitors' center was empty, he'd been able to head to his boat and spend his volunteer time on the water. The air was thick from morning thunderstorms as his boat cascaded along the water, just beneath a cloud of fog. "You can take off early," his supervisor told him earlier that afternoon. But Bruce wanted the opposite. He wanted to push out beyond the shallow waterways and whip around in the area where Lake Pontchartrain met the salt water. He whistled softly and sailed along the edge of the Spanish moss.

Launching from an unimproved site near Crabbing Bridge Road off Highway 11, Bruce felt the familiar rise of joy he experienced every time he took to the water. The airboat glided over the calm bayou, creating gentle waves in its wake. Bruce Carpenter tilted his head to the sky and inhaled. Bayou Sauvage was one of his favorite places in New Orleans. The peace and tranquility reminded him of his hometown of Venice, a little place at the bottom of the boot, as his father often said, referring to Louisiana's shape. Dangerously nestled up against the Mississippi River, it was a portion of Plaquemines Parish that had been the site of many environmental disasters. Hurricane Katrina had almost wiped the place off the map, and after the Deepwater Horizon disaster, his wife, Evie, had asked if they could move.

"Honey, we didn't have nothing left after Katrina. Now the oil done come. This ain't where we grew up," she said in a sweet, quiet voice.

Bruce had considered putting up a fight, but when he looked into Evie's eyes, he gave in and responded, "Let's go near the city, then."

Now Bruce was retired, Della was all grown up, and he was ready to get back to nature. The hurricanes would come, but now they'd just go in-land until it passed. But Evie had found friends and loved heading to the French Quarter and hanging out in all the tourist areas of New Orleans. Bruce always skipped the downtown events, making up excuses about not feeling well, or saying that he was going fishing. Evie knew what he was doing and suggested that he find his happy place. Bayou Sauvage was exactly that. It was his oasis.

As a retired cop, the preserve was happy to have him. Not only was he a fourth-generation fisherman with extensive experience in bayous, but he was also trained as a law officer. Even though the bayou was quiet and safe, the surrounding neighborhoods were not as peaceful. There were several places close to Sauvage that attracted outsiders. It was in Louisiana's best interest to keep the tourist industry safe. Party bus rentals and people traveling to see the Fisherman's Castle increased the number of people in the area, but the preserve had mostly saved this side of the lake, keeping development from taking over the breathtaking landscape. As Bruce and the other volunteers worked on re-foresting projects, the likelihood that Bayou Sauvage would remain natural and uninhibited increased. Even with saltwater intrusion, the place was still wild and free from the unfettered build-up of houses and businesses that had struck other parts of the state.

The airboat skimmed over the water towards St. Tammany Parish. Bruce kept his speed moderate as he drifted through the Rigolets Strait before mashing the accelerator when he emerged in Lake Borgne. The evening was clear and warm, and the clouds from the afternoon thunderstorm had cleared. Seagulls quacked in the background while Bruce daydreamed about the night's festivities. He was excited to see his sweet daughter, Della, who was flying in from Baltimore for a week's stay. Evie was at home whipping up a huge spread that included crawfish etouffee and beignets. After he finished his shift patrolling the bayou, he'd head home for a good time with cousins and friends. Bringing in the New Year with loved ones was so much better than spending the night chasing drunk party goers. *Why didn't I retire earlier,* Bruce thought, a smile creasing his lips. After twenty-five years as a cop, retirement felt like a new lease on life. Now, he volunteered at Sauvage Bayou, took long walks with Evie, and spent evenings in his backyard, watching the moonlit water. Life couldn't have been any better.

Since it was his last round for the night, Bruce headed down toward Shell Beach to get a better look at the breathtaking sunset. Hues of purple and blue filled the sky, pushing Bruce further into a daydream about his childhood.

"This is God's country," Bruce said, easing into a soothing nostalgia. The rest of the world fell away and Bruce barely noticed a small boat in the distance, humming across the water. The occupant threw a hand up while careening by. Bruce caught the name of the vessel, Sea Witch, out of the corner of his eye, but didn't take the time to get a good look at the boat. He threw a hand up, acknowledging the fellow seafarer.

Further downstream, a tugboat hugged the edge of the shore-line. It was a little more than a dinghy, and the boat rocked and bobbed wildly. Bruce, lost in a daydream about the coming evening, didn't notice the potentially dangerous situation. The figures on the boat stumbled and struggled to keep the vessel afloat. Bruce absentmindedly threw up a hand as he cruised past, missing the waving of arms high above one of the tugboat occupant's head.

As he careened away from Shell Beach, he saw an object bobbing in the water close to the shore. A swath of trees and grass divided the lake, but Bruce was sure there was something out there. *Just go home. You ain't a cop anymore,* he thought, but old training dies hard. Bruce steered the boat toward the bobbing item. It was December, so it wasn't a gator, but it was a large... creature of some sort. Bruce fished his wireframe glasses out of his shirt pocket with one hand, holding his gaze and slipping the spectacles back onto his face. The lump was being dragged under the Spanish moss and pulled toward the shore. Continuing the approach, Bruce saw a woman. Her black tank top clung to her chest, her eyes wide. She was fishing something out of the water.

"Don't move a muscle! I tell ya, I'll shoot! Retired cop here! I'm trained and ready!" Bruce yelled, grabbing the Holland and Holland Double Rifle from the rack behind him. The 45 in the tackle box would be better, but the jolt of adrenaline had put him in fight-or-flight mode.

The woman stopped moving, but she continued to clutch the edges of a white shirt that was worn by... a body.

Bruce kept the gun trained on the woman.

"Turn around. Hands up! Face the shore," he yelled, grabbing his cellphone the moment he saw her back.

The small woman slowly let go of the shirt but grabbed it again when the water started pushing the body away from her. Bruce's finger twitched against the trigger, but he held back.

Don't shoot. She doesn't want the body to float away. Would be best for her if it did. Odd, Bruce thought. The woman's shoulders heaved up and down as she scrambled for the body. Bruce yelled for her to get her hands in the air.

"I'll put one in ya if ya hesitate!" he yelled.

The woman reluctantly lifted her arms above her head. Bruce's heart raced as he watched the body slowly drift away.

1

———————

"This isn't going to be good," I muttered.

It had been a rough day. That morning, I'd attended the funeral of a young man I'd mentored. He'd been murdered while trying to help a young mother and her children after a car accident. The senseless tragedy had left me depressed and drained. I'd poured myself a glass of crisp, bubbly peach mead, grabbed an Afghan, and headed to the porch to decompress.

I huddled under a blanket and curled up in the big wooden rocking chair. A chilly breeze picked up every so often, whistling through the bare tree branches and causing a shiver to run through my body. My glass of mead sat on an end table beside me, and the book, *Invisible Man* by Ralph Ellison, rested on my knees, pulled up close to my face. It was just after six and I was finishing up a chapter by way of the porch light when Madalyn Price's blue Rav4 zipped into the driveway. I felt her stare as she approached, but I continued focusing on the book, pretending not to notice her. I didn't look up until she was standing in front of me.

"Did you give it more thought?" Madalyn asked.

"I'm not interested."

"It's a vacation. No work will be done."

"Madalyn, you're always working. Vacation is not in your vocabulary."

"You're right, but that's a pot and kettle kind of thing, right? You're the same way. That's why I'm inviting you. You need a break."

"A lot of things have happened lately. I don't know that I'm up for a trip. A real vacation? Yes. A job disguised as a vacation? No."

"C'mon. We'll stay in the French Quarter, sip on Hurricanes, and chill out for a week. Think about bringing in the New Year in one of the best cities in the country, far away from all our problems. We'll return home ready to start fresh. How much fun would that be? Also, the woman I'm working with is still on the fence about things. I just want to be there in case she changes her mind."

"Why not wait until she's sure?" I asked.

"I've already booked accommodations. Why not just take the trip?"

"How do you know I don't have plans?"

"Is the boyfriend still around?" Madalyn asked.

"I don't know who you're talking about," I said, closing the book on my lap. A chilled wind blew across the porch.

"Pale, bearded guy with long hippie hair. Handsome, abnormally nice, lives in the middle of nowhere? I doubt you've forgotten him."

I felt my cheeks warm as she talked about Brady.

"Madalyn, the answer is no. It was no two weeks ago and nothing has changed," I said, wrapping the blanket tight around my shoulders.

"You know, I'm not just all about work. I know how to relax," Madalyn defended, a slight edge in her voice.

"Maybe next time," I answered, gathering my book and wine glass, and heading for the door.

"Wait," she called after me, catching my shoulder.

"Madelyn, make it quick," I said, stopping and waiting to hear what she wanted.

"I need your help."

I twisted the knob and pushed the front door open.

"It's getting chilly. Come in and tell me what's going on."

Madalyn smiled and followed me inside. I knew it was a mistake, but I had to admit—it intrigued me.

"Thanks for listening," she said. Her voice was warm with enthusiasm.

"I'm listening to your plight. Don't get excited. Can I get you something?" I asked, heading to the kitchen, and putting the kettle on the stove.

"But if you're willing to listen...."

"Relax. Like I said, I'm just listening to what you have to say. That doesn't mean that I'm up for your shenanigans," I warned. It felt like I was scolding a child.

Using the word *petite* to describe Madalyn was an understatement. She was a tiny woman, five feet tall and one-hundred pounds. Yoga and helping young women leave abusive relationships kept her spry. I waited for Madalyn to nod and climb into the recliner before I headed to the kitchen.

"Tea or water?"

"I need to help someone who is stuck in a terrible situation," Madalyn said. Ignoring my question.

"So, why is this different?" I asked, opening a cabinet and reviewing my tea selection.

"She's married to a politician. They also live in Louisiana, so it would be nice to have help."

"How far up the ladder are we talking?"

"State senate. She claims he's already told her she and the

kids will be 'taken care of' if they try to leave," Madalyn said, a hint of disbelief in her voice.

"Claims? You doubt her. Why?"

"Something's off. I don't know what it is, but I'm having a hard time believing her."

I filled my teakettle with water.

"Why get involved if you don't believe her?"

"Because what if I'm wrong?" Madalyn wondered.

I turned on the burner under the kettle and stopped. Madalyn wasn't telling me everything, but I continued to play along.

"Why do you think I can help?"

"You have cop connections," Madalyn said.

"Not in Louisiana."

"But you were a cop and people will listen to you more than they will me. C'mon Sylvia. You know how things work."

"Are you planning on bringing the cops into the situation?"

"No way. The woman I'm helping says they're all crooked."

"Sounds about right from what I've heard about New Orleans, but there are always good cops, no matter how corrupt the agency appears to be. So, what do you need my help with?"

"My team refuses to participate."

"That sounds ominous. I know your team, Madalyn. They're dedicated. If they won't help, something is off. What aren't you telling me?"

"They don't think I should do this one."

I walked to the doorway and stared at Madalyn.

"You know I don't like cryptic. Tell me what's going on."

"The wife claims the husband has a nifty hit man who has taken out political rivals, enemies, and two mistresses."

There it was again. *Claims.* Why didn't Madalyn believe the wife?

The kettle buzzed. I went back to the stove, dropped two green tea bags into mugs, and steeped them in the hot water.

"This might not be one you want to take. If the guy has a long reach, you and your daughter could be in danger. Leave it alone."

"You know I can't, and Kara is fine. She's away at State."

"Madalyn, this is a bad idea and you'll be on his turf. If things go wrong, all of this could be over. So, decide. Do you save the one or the many?

"I thought you were a religious woman. Doesn't your faith tell you that the one is worth going after? Something about a sheep, right?"

Ouch. That was a valid point.

I handed the mug to Madalyn and sat in the recliner catty corner from the couch. A wave of guilt washed over me. I hadn't been to Mass in months.

"Madalyn, I would help if I could, but this doesn't feel right. I think it's too much. I suggest finding another way for her to leave."

"Her husband is connected through the state. I can't go to the police or anything like that."

"But you think I can?" I asked.

"Cops like cops."

I sipped the tea, immediately realizing I'd forgotten to add a few drops of honey.

"What else is there? Does she have anything on him?"

"No idea," Madalyn answered.

"She needs to do some fact finding—something good. After that, she has to leverage her position."

"Sylvia, this woman got married very young. She's been sheltered. I don't think she can do that."

"She can. It's just scary. Look. This isn't something you want to wade into without preparation. I feel for the woman, but this won't be a simple deal where you swoop in like some type of black-ops lady, grab this woman and her kids, and everything just goes back to normal. You need to play the long game on this one. Maybe I can do a little research, but I'm not tagging along. What's her name?" I asked.

"Her name is Krista Broussard. She wants to be out of there as soon as possible. The kids are also starting to think that what their parents have is a regular relationship. According to Krista, the kids are yelling and hitting each other because they think this is the way to communicate."

I took another sip of my tea. The details were vague. Madalyn was hiding something.

"How do you know this woman?" I asked.

"That's irrelevant."

"It sounds like this is more personal than the other cases. I know there's more to it, Madalyn. Talk."

"Okay, but this has nothing to do with what's happening now," Madalyn said. "She got into trouble when she was seventeen. I helped her then."

"When you say got into trouble, are you referring to the archaic, completely unfair characterization of women who become pregnant outside of marriage?"

"Yes. For the record, I was one of those 'in trouble' girls, so I'm not judging. We hid her in a little cabin in rural Tennessee until she had the baby. After that, a relative kept the baby while Krista moved to Louisiana and got married to Nathan Broussard. Several months later, they announced that they'd been married months before and introduced the new baby to the world. Nathan was a well to-do, aspiring politician who is heir to a business built on the back of a sugar plantation."

"Is that still a thing?"

"Sugar plantations? Not in the way they used to be, but yes. The Broussard's own a sugar factory now and they pay wages, so it's different. They also have several other businesses under the Broussard umbrella."

"So, Krista moves into this new situation in Louisiana. I

assume she was from Tennessee. How did she end up with a Louisiana politician?" I asked.

"She'd been in beauty pageants and all that jazz before the pregnancy. She comes from a poor family in Tennessee that recognized the worth of having a beautiful daughter. From the age of four, she was in beauty pageants. After winning several pageants in her teens, Krista headed to a regional competition in Louisiana. Nathan Broussard was one of the judges."

"How long was she in Louisiana for the pageant?"

"One week. Apparently, Nathan Broussard, a well to do aspiring politician and law student, swept her off her feet. The rest is history," Madalyn said.

"Except now he's turned out to be abusive?"

Madalyn hesitated. "I've been told he is abusive. Krista has told me about some incidents, but I haven't been able to verify any of the terrible things she says Nathan does."

"Again, this sounds like a bad idea. The family is rich, has connections, and you seem unsure. Red flags one, two, and three. Don't do it, Madalyn."

I looked up at her clear, calm, ageless face. Unmoved by my advice, she shook her head and smirked.

"I could really use your hand in all of this, Sylvia. This is what we do. We help people," Madalyn said.

"No, that's what you do. I'm not part of the covert association you've got going on. I'm a private investigator and, to be honest, I don't even know if that's going to continue. So, no. I'm out. Not a chance I'm getting involved in this."

Madalyn sipped the tea, set the cup down on the end table next to the couch, and stood. "So much for saving the one. Thanks for the tea and the ear. I'll see myself out."

I considered saying something as Madalyn headed for the door. She'd helped me during inopportune times, moments when my emergencies ran counter to her schedule. Normally, I'd have no problem returning the favor, but the past few months had been full of turmoil. My brain and soul needed a break. I'd even avoided going to the office. Hunkering down at home had provided solace and a reprieve from chaos. Over the past few months, I'd become unsure whether I wanted to return to work. I'd been a cop and a private investigator, but after several shocking and tragic events, I wasn't too keen on uncovering long standing mysteries. But... There was still that undercurrent of intrigue that arrived every time a problem arose. I poured another glass of wine and opened my laptop.

Pictures of Nathan and Krista Broussard were easy to find. New Orleans' local papers seemed to love the attractive, smiling couple. Nathan was tall and handsome, with thick, dark hair and bright brown eyes. Krista was thin and angular with a thick swath of blonde hair folded over the left side of her face. Nathan was a long-term state senator who, having won a seat at the young age of twenty-six, and was now vying for a position at the federal level. Two kids, a political career, a beautiful wife, and based on the pictures of their sprawling mansion, more money than he'd ever need. Nathan Broussard seemed to have it all.

"Why so violent then, Nathan?" I said aloud.

I dug deeper. The Broussards had been well to do since the late 1700s, and no matter what happened, they seemed to have adjusted and shifted their fortune in a way that protected it. The sugar plantation became a sharecropping venture after the Civil War, and eventually, the family invested in oil. Then, during World War One, the factory where the sugar was processed switched and worked on the war effort before transitioning back to sugar production. During the Great Depression, the Broussards had helped their community by giving away a pound of sugar and loaves of bread they didn't sell at market to families. Nathan Broussard had continued the charitable spirit of his great grandparents by working in soup kitchens, venturing out to homeless camps to hand out lunches, and giving away scholarships to underprivileged children. The pictures of him spooning stew into bowls and chatting with the patrons of the homeless center with a big genuine smile on his face didn't line up with a spoiled, rich kid turned politician and abusive husband. I scrolled through links with old newspaper listings of Nathan's community outreach. That was a lot of public relations work for a politician who had consistently won his seat in the state government. Was I jaded in thinking that most politicians only did charitable work for political reasons? I didn't think so, but that made Nathan Broussard's activities seem odd. It showed that he might genuinely care about his constituents. Of course, an abuser often appears to be a great person to the outside world. It's at home that they become monsters.

A quick check of Nathan's family showed that his father had passed away several years ago, but his older brother, Grayson, and his mother, Beth, were still alive. Grayson was a prominent figure in the state's Evangelical Christian community, but according to the company's website, he was also the secretary of the family business, Broussard Incorporated. There were pictures of the brothers and their families planting Bald Cypress trees in the bayou, building homes in lower-income neighborhoods, and scores of images from church functions. I enlarged one image and focused on Krista. Crooked smile and unsure eyes. She wore a look of surprise that seemed to ask, *What have I gotten myself into?*

2

———————

The next morning, I woke up early, strangely energized. I rolled out of bed in the dark, crisp morning, put on sweats, and headed for a run. I took my usual path down Michigan Avenue, through Riverside Park, and up Cross Street. Something about the route felt new, even though I'd run it many times. My legs ached a bit, but the pain was refreshing. Inhaling the frigid air and watching a few snowflakes fall to the ground gave me a visceral appreciation for the impending winter. Christmas decorations filled the few stores that were left on Michigan Ave, but the streets were mostly empty, giving me the feeling that the town was mine to take in and enjoy. By seven, I'd showered, gotten dressed, and walked to work.

My office was on the second floor of an old storefront that dated back to the late 1800s. A few other businesses lined the hallway, and two one-bedroom apartments sat in opposite corners at the back of the building. Seeing the desks—mine and Martin's—covered in dust brought a hint of sadness to my soul. Why did I let things stop me from working? No matter what was going on in my life, work provided purpose—something I desperately needed right now.

Madalyn's visit had prompted me to get back at it. She was reckless, but no matter what, Madalyn Price was going to save lives. She'd been working to help women and children get out of abusive situations for years, and nothing slowed her down. If someone was in need, Madalyn was ready to make a plan and get the victims to safety. It was honorable. Perhaps that was what I needed: A full plate of work to keep my mind off my complicated life. I picked up the phone and dialed the voicemail, hoping that there would be something there. Of course, if you shut down for months at a time, people that needed private investigators would not wait for you to return to work. I hung up after hearing there were no new messages. *Maybe I should help Madalyn,* I thought before pushing the thought out of my mind. While Madalyn was inspiring, she also had a way of finding trouble. She actually went looking for it. Her intentions were good, but she was always playing a dangerous game. If I took a case on now, I wanted it to be low key and not too hard to solve. Satisfied that I would find something better suited to my skills, I wiped the layer of dust off my desk, sat down, and called Martin.

"Hey, can you come in today?"

"Sylvia Wilcox? Is that you," Martin said. His voice was laced with sarcasm.

Martin, the younger brother of my deceased husband, Derek, had been my assistant for years. I still called him my brother-in-law, even though, at this point, it was debatable if that title was correct. Since starting law school the year before, he'd scaled back to part-time, but Martin still made it to the office a few times a month.

"I know. I've been terrible over the past couple of months, but I'm back in the office and I'm ready. You still work for me, right?"

"I do rather like the steady paycheck for minimal or no work."

"I'll take that as a yes. See you soon," I said before ending the call.

Martin showed up thirty minutes later. He was eating a breakfast sandwich from a fast-food joint when he walked through the door.

"It's true. The prodigal employer has returned," Martin said, heading for his desk.

"It's good to see you, too," I said, getting up and giving him a quick side hug.

"So, I know you aren't going to tell me, but how are things with your parents, your brother, and Father Keegan?"

I should have expected the questions, and maybe I did, but I hadn't come up with any replies. A few months before, my life had imploded, leaving me with doubt about everything I thought I knew. The stories I'd told myself about who I was and what my life meant, my family, and some friends, had all turned out to be false. Key parts of my identity were gone, and I didn't know how to feel about that.

"Life goes on. Right now, I'm just taking it day by day. I haven't talked to my parents because they told me not to call them, and Simon... well, we've been out of contact for decades. No need to start that up now."

"Are you sure?"

"Yes. I spent decades of my life looking for Simon, and he was off living and enjoying himself. My life was on hold because I thought we had such a connection, and I loved him so much that I would wake up in the middle of the night calling his name. All the while, he was getting married, having children, working a job, and happy to not have me around."

"You don't know that, Sylvia."

"I do. Remember, we saw it with our own eyes," I sighed

and ran my hands over my face before saying, "Now, since we're talking about dysfunctional families, how is Starla?"

"Not fair."

"Oh, it's fair. How is your mom? Are you speaking with her again?"

Martin sighed. "Not yet. Don't know exactly what to do about that. I can't explain it, but I have this pull to her. She's my mom and even though she's not necessarily a good person, I love her. And I miss her."

I nodded. "You're such a good guy, Martin. Just know that I won't hold it against you if you mended the fence with your mom. She hurt my family, but I'll never ask you to choose between me and your mother."

Starla was a monster in my book, but Martin was the last piece of Derek I had. I wanted to hold on to him.

"What about Father Keegan?"

"What about him?"

"Come on, Sylvia. I know you've talked to him."

"Nope. Haven't been to church lately."

"Really? That's unlike you."

"I've changed, but I'm okay. Now, let's move on."

He nodded his head and said, "What's cooking? Do we have a case or something?"

"I need to run something by you."

"Okay. What's up?"

"Madalyn Price stopped by last night."

"That's probably as much as I need to know. No. Don't do whatever she's asking. You know you will regret it."

"Wait—"

"Listen, Madalyn is stealthy and weird, and you just never know what she's up to. Whatever it is, just say no."

"Hear me out. It's less complicated than it seems."

"Nothing is easy with Madalyn."

I ignored the statement, even though it was mostly true, and said, "So, she called me back when everything went down with Simon and invited me to New Orleans. She said it was a vacation, and she wanted to invite me because she'd seen the news and figured I'd be totally devastated. I wasn't in my right mind, so I agreed to go. But after returning to reality, I realized that there was no way Madalyn was taking a vacation. Everything the woman does is connected to some clandestine operation, so I changed my mind and told her no."

"Great. Then you don't need to tell me anymore. You already know this is going to be messy, so stick to your guns on this one," Martin said.

"But wait. Here's the thing. Madalyn showed up last night and gave me the details and it felt like she didn't trust the woman. Her name is Krista Broussard, and she says she is being abused by her husband. Madalyn seems unsure about the information Krista gave her. Now, it could be that Krista Broussard is struggling so much with the situation and doesn't have an outlet, but I looked up the man and his family, and I don't know if I buy the story Krista gave Madalyn. The fact that the woman is on the fence isn't odd, but something feels off about the whole thing. I know people can have secret lives, but I'm suspicious of the information."

"You should be. Madalyn never tells the entire story. You know that," Martin said, sticking his finger in a mound of dust on his desk before using his forearm to wipe the top, sending a cloud of dust into the air. He took a seat and plopped his feet up on top.

"On the other hand, I don't have any plans for the holidays, and Madalyn's heading to New Orleans the day after Christmas. That could be perfect," I said.

"Why not book a non-working holiday?"

"Well, we haven't been working for the past few weeks and there's nothing on the docket. Technically, I've been on vacation. And she said I could invite Brady."

Martin took his feet off the desk, leaned forward in his chair, and said, "Ah-ha! That's what this is about. You want an excuse to see Brady again."

"No. He came to visit a few months ago. I don't need to see him again any time soon."

"Right, but you want to see him, right? Sylvia, c'mon. Are you moving to Utah, or is he moving to Michigan? Which is it? When is the wedding? The horse is out the gate on this one."

Brady Kepler was a friend who lived in Utah. He'd come along on some of my more interesting cases, and after a debacle of discovering the truth behind my twin brother's abduction, he'd come to town to comfort me. He was indeed a great friend and someone I probably could have a wonderful future with, but I didn't want that much change in my life. Or did I? Some days I did, other times, I took comfort in my single and solitary life.

"You know, fortune favors the brave and the one sheep is worth going after, even if the rest of the flock is safe, and—"

"Sylvia, you won't convince me that this is a good idea, but if you want to head down there with Madalyn, I know you'll be careful. Besides, you might need something to pull you out of your funk."

"You could be right. I went to a funeral yesterday for a kid I knew. He was a great kid trying to do the right thing, and some loser shot him. It hurts in a way that can't be fixed."

"I'm sorry. What happened?"

"There was a car accident. The kid, Jalen, saw the crash and got out to help. The driver that caused the crash got nervous when Jalen said he was going to call the police. He shot Jalen after he dialed 911. Two-thirty in the afternoon in the middle of a busy intersection."

"Disturbing, but that's the city," Martin said. "Now, back to the New Orleans trip. Will you be able to stay out of trouble if Madalyn can't?"

"I'll be careful. I know Madalyn is always working and it won't be a total vacation, but a change of scenery would be good. Basically, she just wants to be in town in case this lady changes her mind and leaves the dangerous situation she's in. If she doesn't do that, Madalyn, Brady, and I will enjoy New Orleans. We'll bring in the New Year and have a good time. This is what I need."

Martin shook his head. "Change is very hard for you, isn't it?"

"What do you mean?"

"You need a vacation, but you just can't take it. Instead, you dive into work."

I grabbed a sheet of paper off my desk and wrote the names of the members in the Broussard family.

"Are you going to school to be a lawyer?"

"Yeah."

"Then stop psychoanalyzing me," I said, tossing the paper at him. "You're not a shrink, and I'm comfortable with my psychosis."

"Just making a casual observation."

"Thanks for caring, but enough of the chitter chatter," I said, winking at Martin. "Earn your keep. Find out everything you can about these people."

THAT NIGHT, I called Madalyn to let her know I wanted to head to New Orleans with her. Her response surprised me.

"I don't know. Things are up in the air."

"Madalyn, you were just at my place, begging me to head down there with you. What happened?"

She was quiet for a moment.

"You're right. I'll text you the address where we're staying. Show up any time after Christmas. Krista isn't sure she wants to leave until sometime next year, but we might as well enjoy the accommodations. I have it booked for two weeks. Are you bringing Brady?"

"Maybe. I'll keep you posted."

I considered calling Brady but decided to send a text message instead. A simple sentence that required nothing more than a yes or no response. *Do you want to go to New Orleans?* I connected my phone to the wall charger and left it sitting on the edge of the couch in the living room before heading to the kitchen to fix dinner. An hour later, I headed back into the living room after finishing a medium rib eye and glanced at the phone.

Anxiety swirled in my stomach as I unlocked the screen and read Brady's text. *Yeah. When?*

I couldn't stop the joy in my heart. I didn't know where things would go with Brady, but I enjoyed his company. Moving to Utah wasn't in the cards—yet—but I felt like there was more to come. My friendship with Brady was one area of my life I was willing to let chart its own course.

3

———————

The day after Christmas, Martin took me to the airport, dropping me off at five-thirty. The frigid temperatures had rolled in on Christmas Eve, bringing with them a storm that had left a slick sheet of ice on the roads.

"Now remember, Madalyn is nice, but she can't really be trusted," Martin said, pulling in front of the airport terminal.

"This is just an innocent trip. Try to relax, Dad," I said, winking before opening the passenger door.

"I can't wait to say I told you so," Martin said, returning an exaggerated wink.

I laughed and grabbed my luggage from the backseat.

"See you in two weeks. Try not to freeze to death," I called out before closing the car door. I rushed inside the terminal and headed to security. The line moved relatively fast, and I ended up drifting to sleep just before the plane boarded. We took off on time, and the ride was smooth. I drifted off about an hour into the trip and woke up when the pilot came over the loudspeaker to announce that we were descending into New Orleans. As Louis Armstrong Airport came into view, I made a silent promise to have a great time. *Forget everything.*

The moment I emerged from the plane, warm, heavy air engulfed my body. Sunshine sparkled through the tree branches and the brightness of the sun brought a smile to my face. The temperature was in the mid-sixties. I immediately shed my thick parka and headed for the baggage claim. The terminal, dubbed the "Jazz Garden", was sleek and attention grabbing. Soft music played in the background, and upscale restaurants lined both sides of the building. I went to rent a car —a sensible, fuel-efficient Honda Accord—and waited for Brady to land. Half an hour later, Brady sent me a text. *Just landed.* I head to the opposite side of the airport and waited in a long, slow-moving line of cars. Brady emerged ten minutes later, dressed in a Hawaiian shirt, beige khaki shorts, and crocs.

"I see you're dressed to impress," I said, leaning across the passenger seat and pushing the door open.

"Just wanted to look the part of a snowbird traveler," he replied, setting his luggage in the backseat. "Sylvia, it's good to see you."

"Same here. Thanks for coming."

We headed for the address Madalyn had given me.

"This place is so... different," Brady commented as we drove by a line of palm trees.

"It's fun and beautiful. We're staying in Bayou St. John. It'll be about a forty-minute walk to the French Quarter, so we'll be close to the action, but not so close that it keeps us up all night. I've got a list of things we can do and most of them are close to the house."

"So, are you working while we're here?" Brady asked.

"Madalyn says no. If anything comes up, I'm guessing it will be something small. So, we'll be relaxing in the sun, sipping drinks, and enjoying our stay."

"This trip is purely a vacation?" Brady asked.

"That's right. No work for the next fourteen days."

"We're going to party as hard as two introverts can."

Laughter filled the car.

"Hopefully, there's a balcony. We can grill and relax," I said.

"Sleep with the windows open," Brady added.

"Maybe try some of those fancy drinks I saw at bars around the airport, go on a ghost tour, and check out museums and historical sites." I stopped at a red light and glanced at Brady.

We locked eyes for a moment. I looked away and said, "We'll bask in the nice, warm weather. Let's be sure to get our fill of snow-free streets and mild temps."

"Agreed. It was snowing when I left Utah. Is Madalyn already here?" Brady asked.

"Yeah, she arrived early this morning. She sent me a text that said she'd be out this afternoon. I'm kind of glad we aren't doing any work during this trip. It's been quite a year. It'll be nice to end it on a positive note."

Louisiana is one of those places the rich love and the poor loathe. The haves and have-nots are on distinct sides of the argument. I expected our accommodations to be adequate and nice, but nothing terribly ritzy. Madalyn Price lived in a modest farmhouse on the outskirts of Ann Arbor, which also served as her yoga studio. When she'd invited me to New Orleans, I expected to stay at a place outside of the city. It shocked me when I looked up the directions to the house on DeSoto Street.

"This is a great location, but I can't imagine how much it cost to secure this place."

"Things do look rather fancy around here," Brady observed.

I'd been in the area during previous trips to New Orleans. The house was a few blocks from Frontier Park. The Bayou St. John neighborhood was walkable with Esplanade close by and a few sights to see along the way. We pulled in front of a gray stucco house with two sets of double doors donned in plantation shutters—one set downstairs that served as the front door, and one set upstairs that opened to a small patio.

"I love the architecture," Brady said as we parked in front of a wrought-iron gate.

"It really is something. Wow! Madalyn has outdone herself," I agreed, parking and staring at the house in awe.

The house was centrally located. We were within walking distance of restaurants, groceries, historical markers, the streetcar, and everything else.

"What does something like this cost here?" Brady asked.

"A lot. I guess being an excessive workaholic is paying off for Madalyn."

The need to investigate fell away. Suddenly, I wasn't concerned with the Broussard clan, the chaos I'd lived through during the past year, or anything else.

"Let's get in there," I said, dreamily staring up at the house.

We grabbed our luggage and headed inside. The house had an open floor plan. Large windows allowed optimum light into the living and dining rooms, and an elegant and historic wood staircase led to the second level of the house. Madalyn had left the windows open and the long, cream curtains were gently billowing in the breeze. The place smelled of lavender with hints of coffee in the background, with *Make yourselves at home!* scrawled on a whiteboard on the refrigerator. Madalyn was not a particularly warm person. She'd always been about business when we interacted, but this message showed a different side of her. Perhaps, this time, she really was serious. This was a bona fide vacation.

We headed upstairs and claimed bedrooms opposite one another. Each room had queen-sized beds that sat high off the ground, bureaus, and nightstands. I dropped my bags on the floor and fell back on the bed, sinking into the mattress.

This is what I need, I thought as I allowed my mind to go blank.

"This place is great, but we didn't come here to lie around,"

Brady said, standing in the room's doorway. "It's midday. What's the first stop?"

I sighed. The bed was so comfortable, but Brady was right. We needed to head out and be the tourists that we were.

"Just a few more minutes," I said, rolling over onto my side.

"Thirty minutes. Then we're out of here."

"An hour. I have to get ready."

Twenty minutes later, I was up ironing a turquoise summer dress. I'd brought along a white shawl for my shoulders, but the weather was warmer than had been forecasted. Even so, I would take it. I styled my hair into soft, flipped curls, struggled to apply eyeliner, and dug a pair of boots that matched my dress out of the suitcase.

"Wow! You look amazing. I feel so under dressed," Brady said. He had changed into a green shirt with a John Deere tractor on the front, faded blue jeans, and a pair of black and brown cowboy boots. His long, blonde hair was pulled into a ponytail at the nape of his neck.

"You look... western, but it's a good look for you. Let's see what we can see," I said, looping my arm through his.

We headed out into the warm afternoon, strolling toward the French Quarter. Pockets of people were scattered along the streets and the crowds thickened the closer we got to Bourbon Street.

"Looks like a party around here," Brady said.

"Yeah, there always seems to be a party here. Each time I've been here, something similar to Mardi Gras is going on, no matter what time of year it is. It's not a place I think I could live, but I enjoy spending a few days here."

"Really? That surprises me. You aren't much of a partier."

"No, but I do like a festive atmosphere now and then. Yes, I'm a total introvert, but sometimes I enjoy watching my fellow humans partake in fun."

"I understand. Sometimes the shop gets lonely, and I have

to head out and find people to socialize with. Thanks for inviting me."

I nodded. Brady owned a mechanic shop that he ran in the back of his home in Utah. We'd met a few years ago when I was working a case in the desert. Over the years, we'd grown closer, and now, we were in a gray area. Friends. Definitely. Something more? Maybe.

"Sure. Glad you could make it," I said.

"There's music everywhere."

"Yeah. Feels like some type of Disneyland for adults." I felt my head bobbing to the music.

As we neared the French Quarter, the liveliness of the area took over. Music that reminded me of the book, *Ragtime*, rang out in the streets. We visited the local haunts and strolled around until we came to Café Du Monde.

"I think there's some kind of law that we have to have beignets," I said, grabbing Brady's arm and pulling him into the café. The undercurrent of chatter filled our ears as we ordered the pastries and coffee. We headed to the patio where a cool breeze washed over us as we took seats near a white, wrought-iron fence.

"I love the architecture," Brady said.

"It is a beautiful mix of French and Spanish that's later tempered with Americana. There are some scars from Katrina, but still plenty to love. I forgot how enchanting this place was," I said, leaning back in the patio chair. The tension that usually sat in the back of my neck had disappeared. It felt good to be on a real vacation.

"There's a question I need to ask."

"Okay," I said. "Ask me anything."

"What's going on with your brother?"

I threw my head back and sighed. "So, you chose the one question I refuse to answer?"

"Sylvia, you were in a bad state the last time I saw you. I've been worried sick. You don't call regularly and avoid the tough conversations through text. I came to Michigan when you needed someone because I care. I just want to know that your day-to-day existence isn't like what I saw a couple of months ago."

"You're right. I don't think I ever thanked you for coming to Michigan. Thank you so much for being there for me," I said. My stomach was curling up in knots.

"Actually, you thanked me, Sylvia. But I want to know how you are now."

Things were getting much more serious than I wanted them to be at that point. There were unresolved feelings between Brady and me, but I didn't want to deal with that, or any of the baggage I'd left in Michigan.

"I owe you an update and I'll give you one. Just—Let's not get too far into this. I want to relax and have fun, okay?"

Brady nodded his head.

"Okay. I returned to work a little while ago and I'm leaving all that stuff with Simon in the past. That's really all there is to tell."

"You haven't talked with your brother since you saw him in Gary?"

"No. I think it might be too late to mend that wound. We've been apart for so long and only one of us was looking for the other."

"What about your parents?"

"It's complicated."

"So, you're just avoiding all that stuff?"

"For now. I just need a break from all the noise. I will deal with all of that in time."

"Time is limited."

Fair point, but I wasn't ready to deal with the debacle that was my family.

"Brady, you're the best. I appreciate your friendship, but if it's too overbearing, turn me down," I said. My voice was smooth and even, but I was screaming inside, *Lay off, Brady!*

"Alright. Did I mention that I recently started seeing someone?"

I gripped the edge of my Coffee Au Lait. "Um... That's good. I mean, yeah. Congrats." My face warmed and my heart quickened.

"I think you might be blushing. It's a joke, Sylvia. I'm still free as a bird... For now."

Brady roared with laughter.

"Whatever you decide," I said, feeling a wave of calm.

"You say that, but your face says something else," he laughed.

"Very funny, Brady," I said, quickly switching the subject. "So, here's the thing. The situation with my brother and parents is very complicated. I don't know how to deal with it, so I'm just letting it sit for a while."

"Time passes fast. It's best to move on while you can. Some people would give anything to have their missing loved one back. Do you remember that feeing? Well, now you've got your brother. Don't miss out on knowing who he is."

I took a drink of my coffee and sighed.

"I know you're right."

"And the rest of it. Sylvia, if you have another chance... in other areas of your life, take them."

The only subject more complicated than my family was my friendship with Brady.

"Brady, when Derek died, I accepted the fact that I'd never be able to love again. So now, I just do what I can and try not to have regrets. It's scary to think about being with someone and having history repeat itself. Derek kept so many things from me. I'm tired of secrets and relationships always have them."

Brady smiled. "I guess we've changed the subject."

I took a sip of my coffee, realizing that I'd switched to

making excuses about why I wasn't currently in a relationship. That's what this was really about, wasn't it?

"I thought you were moving the conversation in this direction," I said.

"Here's what I have to say on that. Sylvia, if you miss out on people while they're here, you can't help but have regrets. So, when the day comes and you can no longer talk to your brother, or anyone else that you've passed up on, you will regret it. Utah is still beautiful and safe. There's still an extra bedroom you could turn into an office and, to be honest, there are a lot of weird cases you could investigate there."

My cheeks warmed. I wasn't sure how to respond, so I said, "Trust and connections are tough for me. This whole thing with Derek, his mom, my parents, and my brother... Even my priest had some secrets with my parents I didn't know about. It made me realize that everything I think I know might be false."

"That's one way to look at it, but maybe some of it is a misunderstanding. Maybe all those people were doing the best they could all the time. Mistakes happen. Sometimes, we can't undo the harm they cause, but that doesn't mean we should give up. As long as you have breath in your lungs, you've got another chance. Don't waste it."

MADALYN WAS at the house when we returned.

"Welcome to New Orleans, you two. Are you ready to have a great time?" Madalyn reached out and gave me an awkward hug. Her eyes were bright with excitement. I'd never seen her behave this way.

"Thank you so much for inviting us. This is nice," I said.

"We need to do a swamp tour and a ghost tour. We must do both," Madalyn said, pure glee in her voice.

I was shocked, but she was actually behaving like a tourist.

She seemed genuinely happy. A pair of large, dark sunglasses were perched atop her head and her hair, which I'd never seen in anything but a no-nonsense bun, hung loosely below her shoulders. She was wearing gold capris and a short-sleeved, cream shirt. Her elegant, strappy, gold sandals revealed perfectly sculpted, bright red toenails.

"We need to throw a cemetery tour on the agenda, too," I added.

"Wow. You two have been researching this place," Brady said.

"Life has been tough this year. We're going to finish it on a cheerful note," Madalyn said.

I wasn't sure what had happened to Madelyn, but she seemed even more ready to be done with the year than I did.

"This is really a vacation?" I asked.

"I told you," Madalyn said. "This is fun, fun, fun. We're close enough to downtown to walk to things. I've got all the fixing for mimosas, and the fridge is stocked. We can grill something or head to a restaurant. What do you guys think?"

Brady and I looked at each other. This was so strange, but it looked like it was time to loosen up.

"Let's head back downtown and do one of those ghost tours," I said.

"Yes! Tomorrow we'll do the swamp tour," Madalyn said, a smile in her voice.

"We can also look around for other stuff while we're downtown tonight. There's always something to do in this place."

"Should we drive? We might be really spooked. Walking home might be scary." Madalyn's eyes were wide.

"Are you serious?" I said, laughing.

"You're not the least bit scared of all the voodoo and stuff like that down here?"

"No, Madalyn. I'm not afraid of ghosts. I'm over the age of eight and know such things don't exist."

"Oh, really?" Brady chimed in.

I looked at Brady before turning back to Madalyn.

"You two believe in ghosts?"

"I believe there are things I can't explain. Could there be a ghost out there, maybe. Bigfoot? Maybe. Loch Ness Monster... Probably not, but I'm not completely ruling it out," Brady said.

Madalyn and I laughed. My shoulders sank with ease. The constant tension in between my shoulders disintegrated. This was a real vacation. It was time to relax.

4

———————

We ordered tickets for the ghost tour and walked downtown, enjoying the humid night. We waited near a bar named Rocky's for the ghost tour host, chatting with other people who had also gathered for the event. By the time the tour started, there were close to thirty people ready to head off into the darkness.

Two hosts showed up. One was a stocky man named Larry with spiked gray hair and a white beard, and the other was a tiny lady named Sheena, who had a shaved head and a nose ring. They greeted the crowd, ran through safety instructions, and checked for signed release forms before the tour began.

The air was warm and inviting while being simultaneously foreboding and spooky. We began our tour at the Mississippi River, where the tour host shared stories about the levee and life before it was built.

"Some have reported spirits of those who drowned in the aftermath of hurricanes moving through this area," the host told us.

Our next step was the Lalaurie Mansion, where we spent a significant amount of time listening to stories of paranormal events, but several assaults and a murder were also mentioned. I got lost in the scenery instead of listening to the host, but now and then, I heard a bit of information that caused me to chuckle. Brady and Madalyn seemed to be closely following along with the rest of the tour. The host, with the long, white beard that reached to the middle of his chest did most of the talking. His voice was a deep, guttural tone that fit the brutal tales he was spinning. He walked with a slight limp, which added to the presentation, and his voice was raspy and cautious, making him a brilliant choice for telling ghost stories. But the tales he'd told so far had been full of clichés; I couldn't help but be a little disappointed.

"This is so good. I'm glad we're doing this," Madalyn whispered. I nodded and tried to look interested as we shuffled along with the crowd. We came to the entrance of a cemetery.

"Enter at your own risk," Larry bellowed loudly. The crowd hesitated as the two hosts walked into the cemetery. "You don't get to hear the story unless you come inside."

Brady grabbed my arm, eyes wide, and whispered, "Are you scared?"

I smirked and pulled my arm away. "Terrified."

The three of us moved inside of the gates of the cemetery with the rest of the crowd. We inched past giant tombs. The hosts motioned for the crowd to come to the middle of the cemetery. Once there, he turned to face us, immediately launching into a story.

"One of the souls that roams this area of the city is named Moses. He escaped a plantation in the late 1700s, but he wasn't able to get his wife and children out. He'd worked on the plantation of a prominent family... We never say whom, but that family was terrible to Moses. Cruel and unjust punishment was doled out for fun. If a slave was caught escaping, they were tortured, and their heads were put atop stakes in the ground around the plantation. This was done to warn others they would meet the same fate if they tried to leave. But Moses was smart and patient. He waited until the prominent, slave-owning family was holding a wild party. Everyone was drunk and belligerent, and Moses saw his chance to run. He told his wife and kids he'd be back for them. They kissed and hugged him, and Moses took off. He wanted to get settled elsewhere before he took his family, so he headed off and became what a Maroon. Maroons were slaves that escaped and lived in places slave owners didn't go. Some lived on sections of the plantations the slave owners were unfamiliar with. Others took shelter in swamps and caves, which is what Moses did. He stayed in a cave by day, hunting and mingling by night. Once he was established in the community, he decided it was time to get his family. One night, Moses went back to the plantation, determined to get his family out. Unfortunately, he was shot and killed. His wife was so grief stricken that she worked the roots on the slave-owning family. She wished them great folly and cursed the descendants. Philomena stated that the youngest son over five generations would die before his 35th birthday."

"If he doesn't tell us their name, I don't think it happened," I whispered to Brady, whose eyes were wide with shock.

"Let's hear the rest of the story before we say it's fake," he whispered back.

"You know I like to fact check things."

"Great. But let's get the entire story first."

"Quiet," Madalyn whispered.

"Philomena eventually took her kids and they become Maroons, as well. It is said that a spirit led her and the kids to the same cave Moses lived in. And to this day, Moses still refuses to pass on to the next life. He's still looking for his wife, Philomena. He's caught somewhere between this life and the next," Larry continued.

"Are there any descendants of Moses left in New Orleans?" I

asked. The tour guide titled his head. I guess questions weren't common.

"Ma'am, we disclose nothing about the families."

"But you told us his first and last name."

The man folded his arms over his protruding belly.

"Ain't none of them left around here," he said, clearly annoyed.

I was rolling my eyes when a blood-curdling scream erupted behind us.

The crowd scattered. Brady grabbed my hand, and I took hold of Madalyn's elbow. We rushed away from where the scream came from, scrambling with the other patrons. Over the screeching and frightened yelling, a voice called out.

"Folks, folks. It's okay. It's part of the show. Sorry to scare ya'll like that," Larry laughed. "The questions came right before the scream was supposed to happen. Please come on back ya'll."

The three of us looked at one another and giggled.

"Not so fake when a scream scares you," Brady said, giving me a light nudge with his elbow.

"I've been found out," I said, giving myself over to the fun.

"I wonder how much money this ghost tour generates?"

"Shhh," Brady said, holding his index finger up to his lips." Sylvia, I'm trying to hear. This is pretty spooky."

I smiled, shook my head, turned to Madalyn, and whispered, "I think Brady is into this."

Madalyn shot me a look.

"What?"

"Quiet, Sylvia. You're gonna make me miss the rest of the story. I want to hear how this ends."

I suppressed a giggle, realizing that both Brady and Madalyn were really digging into the ghost stories. I walked along in disbelief, half listening and half taking the reactions of the other people on the tour. The nervous gasps and whispers were all in good fun, but I was getting a little bored. Imagining a ghost floating through the city streets and attacking someone in a crowd without anyone else seeing the entity was just too unrealistic.

Back at the rental, the story of Moses and his family was all the rage.

"I never heard of a Maroon," Brady said.

"It was a thing. There were revolts, and I think a community of Maroons was established in St. Malo at some point."

"Fascinating. Must have been a harsh existence," Madalyn said.

"And yet, it was better than the conditions they'd lived under before," I added.

"I wonder who the family is that is still living with the curse," Madalyn said.

"He said it was a prominent family. Bet super sleuth Sylvia can find out," Brady added.

"You two are so taken with this craziness. I will gladly prove to both of you that there is no such thing. We heard a story tonight, but I will look for info on the topic. Shouldn't be too hard to a find prominent family in the area that has consistently lost the last son of the family before the age of thirty-five."

"What about Moses? I wonder if we can find some of his descendants?" Brady said, pulling out his phone.

I shook my head. "You two really want to look for some fictional characters? I guess that is one way to spend a vacation."

"You know what they say, the devil's greatest trick is convincing us he doesn't exist," Madalyn said.

"Oh. Now you're religious? I thought I was the only one out of the three of us that had a religious slant."

"I don't dabble in the organized form of religion, but I know there is good and evil in the world. It doesn't have to be something supernatural, but evil is real," Madalyn explained.

It was a refrain I'd heard many times, but what did it mean? Were we to believe that there was a brooding, dark force behind the tragedies of the world? Was there a quiet battle between good and evil raging in the background whenever a bad choice was made? What about when a good choice was made? What were we to take from this sentiment?

"Sylvia should have some answers for us. She's the religious person here," Brady said.

"Yes, but my faith is built on the concept that most things are a mystery—including why evil exists."

"That brings us to the question…Why not have the world be all good?" Sylvia asked.

"Because you'd never be able to appreciate the goodness if it was all you knew," Brady answered.

"Yes," I said. "That is my perception on the matter."

"And on that Sunday school note, I'm going to let you two battle this one out. I have a run to make," Madalyn said.

I looked at the clock on the wall. It was eleven-forty.

"Don't ask, okay?" she said.

Knowing that Madalyn was very private, I let it go. Besides, if she had a secret beau somewhere in the Crescent City, who was I to pry?

5

We spent the next few days going on swamp tours, visiting museums, and doing as many touristy things as we could. By the time New Year's Eve arrived, we were all having a wonderful, relaxing time.

We made plans to walk to the river and watch fireworks that day. Madalyn took off early in the morning and Brady and I lounged around the house and on the patio until a rainstorm swept in. The downpour lasted for about half an hour before the sky cleared. Around five, we got dressed and started preparing for a night out on the town. I sent Madalyn a text message around six, letting her know we planned to leave around eight. I began to worry when I hadn't heard from her by seven.

"Well, she's a grown woman," Brady said.

"You're right. She's an adult, but it's unlike her not to keep her word. She usually responds quickly."

"Maybe she's lost track of time," Brady said.

"Yeah. Maybe," I said, but that wasn't how Madalyn operated.

Brady and I waited until 8:30 for Madalyn to show up. After several calls to her phone went unanswered, we headed out.

"I do not know what she's doing, but I'm willing to bet it has something to do with the case she mentioned."

"Sylvia, she's a big girl. I bet she just had a change of plans. Let's just head to the river," Brady said.

I looked at my phone one last time before slipping it into my purse. Keen to walk to the French Quarter, I dressed in layers, throwing a sweatshirt over my tank top and slipping on a pair of comfortable shoes. The streets were busy with cars headed on the way to New Year's Eve festivities. The sidewalks were also crowded with party goers who'd chosen to walk instead of drive. Strolling through the warm New Orleans night had a gothic feel to it. A few ghost tours passed by us as we entered the French Quarter, and revelers were out in full force. The air was thick and vibrant, with crowds forming on street corners. We stopped by a stand and bought a couple of beers before heading closer to downtown.

"The fireworks will be visible from here, I think."

"I'd like to make it to the riverfront. I love that light that shines off the water, but let's take our time getting down there," Brady said.

We meandered through the streets, taking in the sights and sounds while sipping our drinks. Brady held onto my waist when we passed through tightly packed streets, and anyone who saw us would have assumed we were a couple. It felt good being with Brady, and his hands gently guiding me through the crowded street weren't entirely unwelcome.

We came upon a group of boys drumming on empty plastic buckets. People danced in the street and tossed coins into the straw hats at their feet.

"Fancy a dance?" Brady asked.

I thought back to another time when we'd danced our hearts out at a ballroom party at a ski resort.

"Hope you can keep up," I said, throwing his arm over my head and twirling around.

We swayed to the drumbeat for a while, laughing and stopping to take sips of beers. It was fun, and I felt free from all obligations. We danced until we were tired, ordered up a few more beers, and as the clock moved toward midnight, we stumbled toward the Mighty Mississippi.

"Do we dare try one of those Hurricanes everyone's sipping on?" Brady asked.

"Well, why not?" I asked, laughing, and looping my arm through Brady's.

The Hurricane was sweet and strong. We sipped them from long, plastic tubes that were shaped like straws. The moon illuminated the packed pier as we stumbled closer to the edge. I'd taken off my sweatshirt and tied it around my waist. Now that we were close to the water, a cool breeze caused me to shiver. Brady put his arm around me and rubbed the goosebumps off my shoulder. I considered pulling away. We were just friends, but it was comforting, and I had a bit of a chill.

The fireworks started around eleven-thirty. They were loud, with patriotic music playing in the background. The crowd roared with appreciation as the sky lit up with brilliant colors. I felt a rush of wonderment as I stared at the colored sky.

"This is great. Thanks again for inviting me," Brady said, gently pulling me into the crook of his neck.

I pulled away and held up my drink.

"Five minutes until the New Year," I said, toasting Brady.

As we smiled at one another, a wave of anxiety rose in my chest. Would we kiss at midnight? Would that be inappropriate? I diverted my eyes, took a drink, and let the moment unfold without worry. That was when I felt my phone buzz in my purse, giving me an excuse to prevent anything from happening.

"It's a local number. There might be something wrong at

the house or something like that. I better get this," I said, walking away from the riverfront and plugging one ear with a finger before answering the phone.

"Sylvia, I need help."

"Madelyn? What's going on?"

"I'm in jail in the 7th district," Madalyn's voice cracked as she spoke.

"Okay. Don't worry. I will figure this out. You won't be in there long."

"Call Carson Stark."

"Yes. Of course. I'll call him."

I hadn't heard Carson's name in a long time. I'd worked a case for him several years ago.

I knew it wasn't a good idea to have a real conversation on the jailhouse phone, so I stopped myself from asking more questions.

"I'm going to call Carson, okay? Don't worry. We'll figure this out."

"I know. Thanks"

Madalyn hung up. I froze for a minute and rushed back to the riverfront.

"Brady, we've got to go."

"But it's only one minute until midnight," Brady said, inching closer to me, slipping an arm around my waist.

"Madalyn's in jail."

"I wasn't expecting to hear that. What happened?"

"I'm not sure," I said, grabbing Brady's hand.

We pushed through the crowd of people while the fireworks went off in the background. We rushed through the streets, my head in an alcohol haze. Weaving around kissing couples and drunken college students, we made our way back to the condo.

"What happened?" Brady asked as we ran toward DeSoto Street.

"I don't know much. She's in jail, so we couldn't talk. She just told me she needs a lawyer."

As soon as we were back at the house, I opened my laptop and pulled up a local news station website. *Popular Politician Killed Near Bayou Sauvage Refuge.* I read a few lines and stopped when I reached the part about a female suspect being arrested.

"This article is about...a politician that was murdered. A female suspect has been arrested. Originally, Madalyn was going to help the wife of a politician leave her unhappy marriage. I think this article might be referring to Madalyn's arrest," I said.

"Are you sure?"

"Not one hundred percent sure, but it's quite a coincidence if this isn't why she's in jail. She's at the 7th precinct. This guy is a prominent politician and now he's dead. It's going to be on all the news stations by morning. I have to get in touch with her daughter and Carson Stark before that happens."

Brady read over my shoulder.

"The article doesn't mention the victim's or suspect's names?"

"No, but I bet that will all change over the next few days. It's a holiday, so we probably won't see Madalyn's name released for a while, but Nathan Broussard is a state senator. The media might jump on the sensational nature of the crime."

"Why would Madalyn be with this guy?" Brady asked.

"She must have gone through with the job. Maybe he interfered when she was trying to get his wife out. This could be self-defense. Initially, we were supposed to come down here and help Nathan Broussard's wife, Krista, get away from him. He is allegedly an abuser, but Madalyn seemed to not believe Krista Broussard's claims. Madalyn told me we weren't going to help until sometime next year."

"Something must have changed. Maybe she met with him to find out if he truly was an abuser," Brady said.

"Madalyn rarely does that, but this time around, she didn't seem to believe Krista Broussard. I guess that's something to consider. Madalyn wants me to call Carson Stark."

"You worked a case for him once, right?" Brady asked.

"Yeah. He and Madelyn are still close because their children have a common half-sister. Madalyn might need his help to secure an excellent attorney if things go that far, which I assume they will. If they've got enough evidence to hold her, she's not just going to walk out of there without a fight. Martin did a write up on Nathan Broussard and his family for me. I didn't pay too much attention to it because it didn't matter once Madalyn told me the gig was off. But he's got a lot of history and connections in this town," I said.

"Madalyn's an outsider. If she's being accused of murdering an important local figure, the odds of her getting out at all are slim—even with a good attorney," Brady said

"This is crazy. I don't know how long I can stay here, but I wouldn't feel right leaving Madalyn in jail down here."

"I've got an assistant working in the shop. I can stay here and work with you."

"Brady, I can't ask you to do that for Madalyn."

"I wouldn't be doing it for Madalyn," he said.

Tension rose in my throat. It was such a nice offer, but didn't it suggest something more than friendship? I shook off the thoughts about my social life and tried to focus on Madalyn.

"Let's try to get some rest. We've been drinking and this thing with Madalyn is so out of the blue. Let's reconvene in the morning," I said, heading off to my room.

6

———

I tossed and turned for a few hours before giving up on sleep around five that morning. My head spun as I tried to recall the events of the night before. I wasn't hungover, but my head was fuzzy. I sat up in the bed, allowing my eyes to adjust to the predawn light, and waited for clarity.

"Madalyn," I said, remembering the phone call from the night before. Madalyn was still sitting in a jail cell. All I could think about was Louisiana's infamous Angola Penitentiary. While not all prisons in Louisiana were like that, I still didn't like the idea of Madalyn being incarcerated in a state with such a notorious penal record. I got out of bed, slipped on sweatpants and a t-shirt, and headed downstairs where I started a pot of coffee, opened my laptop, and refreshed the local news station's website. The top story was the murder of Nathan Broussard. I clicked on the video.

"While most people were preparing to celebrate the New Year, Senator Nathan Broussard was taking his last breath near Bayou Sauvage." The reporter paused for effect. A clip of the Bayou Sauvage flashed across the screen before she continued.

"The good senator, philanthropist, and beloved native son

was found floating in the water, and even though the police have a suspect in custody, they are very tight-lipped about the details. We do not know what the cause of death is at this point, but there is a suspect in custody. The police have told us not to expect a statement any time soon."

I paused the video and searched for articles. Most repeated the information from the video, but one website had taken a different route by reaching out for comment from Nathan's brother and one of his campaign aides. I clicked on the clip labeled *Grayson Broussard reacts to brother's murder.*

"My baby brother didn't deserve this. We are going to make sure that justice is served, but right now, we just need ya'll to pray for our family. That's all," Grayson Broussard said, choking back sobs.

A small picture at the bottom of the article showed a baby-faced man wearing a somber look. Beneath the photo a short caption read: *Holden Timmons, Senator Broussard's aide said that the senator took off early that day to meet a friend.*

"We never thought that would be the last time we saw him. It was just a normal day. We didn't think anything about him leaving early because it was New Year's Eve. Figured he had plans for the evening," Holden said.

The rest of the article was a rehash of the first video I'd watched. I jotted down the names of Nathan's brother and the campaign aide on a sheet of paper. The Holden Timmons quote was followed by a second picture of him wiping away a tear. I pushed the laptop away and decided it was time to call Carson.

Carson Stark was a former client, but the last time I'd seen him, we'd met for beers. It had been uncomfortable, and I'd decided that a friendship with Carson wasn't a good idea. His Type A personality and brooding mood were more than I could take in a social setting. We were just too different.

"Hello?" Carson said, picking up after the third ring.

"Carson. It's Sylvia Wilcox."

"What can I do for you?" Carson asked, sounding groggy.

"Hey, sorry to wake you, but I'm in New Orleans with Madalyn and I've got some bad news."

"Sylvia, I just got off work a few hours ago. What's going on?" Carson said. His voice had turned cold and impatient.

Carson is a surgeon. I chalked up his impatience to stress and exhaustion.

"Madalyn's in jail. She told me to call you."

"What?" he said. His voice was suddenly full of alarm. "What do you mean she's in jail?"

"I think she's being held on a murder charge."

"You're not making sense. Madalyn is in jail?" Carson said, his voice raising.

"Sadly, yes. It's New Year's Day, but I'm going to head over to the precinct. I don't think we'll be able to do much, but I'll take whatever information I can get."

"What happened? Who is she accused of murdering?"

I considered how much I should tell Carson. I wasn't sure how much he knew about Madalyn's covert activities.

"I'm still getting the facts," I said.

"Okay. I'll let Kara know. Do you think she'll get bail?"

"Not sure. If she does, it won't be until next week."

"Call me with the amount. I'll wire the money. She'll also need a lawyer. I might have someone in mind."

"Really?"

"Yeah. She'll have the best. Whatever it takes."

Carson was much more eager to help than I thought he would be. Clearly, there was more to his connection with Madalyn than I thought. I reassured him I'd keep him updated, hung up, and called Martin.

"Happy New Year, Syl. How's New Orleans?" Martin asked.

"You remember how you said I shouldn't go on vacation with Madalyn?"

"Yeah," Martin said. "It didn't take a psychic to figure out this was going to go bad. What happened?"

"Madalyn's in jail."

"For what?" Martin asked.

"Murder."

"Yikes. That's much worse than anything I thought would happen. I knew it would take a turn, but I never imagined this would be the result. Who is she accused of murdering?"

"Nathan Broussard."

"The politician? That's terrible. She's never getting out. From what I've found, this guy is a hometown hero around the state. Did you look at the info I gave you?" Martin asked.

"I took a glance. From what I saw, you're totally right. She's not getting out if they've got enough evidence to hold her."

"So, what are you going to do?"

"Madalyn wanted me to call Carson Stark, so I did that. He says he'll get her the best attorney he can find. That might change the story."

"Why's that?" Martin asked.

"The only thing that beats a money man is another money man. An excellent lawyer will pick apart a case until there isn't anything left."

"And let me guess. You're going to be on the ground gathering information to arm Carson."

"Have you heard about prisons in the southern United States? I can't leave Madalyn down here. We've got to get her out."

"Okay. What do you need from me?"

"Forward me the information you found about Broussard. I made the mistake of leaving the file at the office."

"Slacker," Martin said.

"I thought all bets were off for the job, but yes. I was Louisiana dreaming, and not paying attention."

"Hey, be careful down there. You and Brady don't need to put your necks on the line for Madalyn."

"It's always worth going after the one sheep that leaves the flock," I said, remembering how it had taken Madalyn to remind me of that.

"Okay. Well, when the biblical stories start, it's time for me to go. I'll email the info straight away."

Brady and I hopped into the car and headed to the precinct. It was an old, dilapidated building well beyond its Gothic days of glory. I cringed to think that my friend was in one of those jail cells. We parked in a garage and headed across the street.

"Hello. I'm here about Madalyn Price," I said to the officer behind the counter.

"Yeah. We got her all right, but you ought to know that from the news, she ain't going nowhere, so I don't know why you came."

The officer was short, with a potbelly and a balding head. He hiked up his belt around his belly button, only to have it slide back down. His face was smug, and it seemed to give him a sense of satisfaction to tell me we wouldn't be able to get Madalyn out.

"I need to know what's going on here. My name is Sylvia Wilcox, and I'm a private investigator."

"We've got a private detective here," the officer said, loud enough for the other cops in office to hear. He let out a chuckle and said, "Well, I don't know where you from, but it don't mean nothing down here."

I knew he was right, but sometimes, officers would cut me some slack.

"I understand. But it would be great if you could help me out."

"She'll probably have bail after the holiday. Might take a while, so don't hold your breath."

"Hey, listen. I used to be a cop. Detroit Police Department. Any information you can share with me would be great."

"If you was a cop, you know we ain't got a lot of information at this stage. We just know your friend killed somebody and she ain't getting out of here. That's the story. Happy New Year's."

The officer leaned back in his chair and put his hands behind his head with a satisfied look on his face.

Brady came up behind me and said, "Hey, listen. We just want to find out what's going on with our friend so we can help. Whatever you can tell us would be great." The officer behind the counter loosened up a bit. He stood, looking at me and then at Brady.

"Ya'll going to need a lot of help. It's going to be on the news, so I guess it can't hurt me telling you. One of our state senators has been murdered. He's a real prominent guy and ain't nobody gonna like that he's gone. Your friend just happened to be there. Did she do it? Looks like it from where I'm standing. We don't know what happened, but she's not going anywhere. Don't think that you should count on bail—even after the holiday."

"Thank you," Brady said, pulling my arm and leading me toward the door. I reluctantly followed him out to the car. We rode back to the condo in silence. I parked the car in the driveway and sighed.

"Not sure what to do right now. I guess we just try to figure out what happened, where Madalyn was that day, and whatever else we can scratch up about Nathan."

"Maybe the judge will be lenient and let her have bail," Brady said once we were inside.

"If they set bail, it's going to be a fortune. This is a nightmare. I knew I couldn't trust Madalyn to just come to New Orleans and be normal."

"Let's just go over what we know. Madalyn didn't murder this guy," Brady said.

"Right, but someone did, and she was the only one there. Let's check to see what other details the press has come across."

We headed back to the house and got to work.

I opened my laptop and scrolled through the headlines. One jumped out at me.

Suspect in Broussard's Murderer Had Twenty Thousand in Cash

"I hope this isn't true," I said, turning to Brady.

He walked over and stared at the screen. "That doesn't look good."

"It says, 'Nathan Broussard's killer had twenty-thousand dollars in her pocket. The suspect, who has not yet been identified, is reportedly being uncooperative with police. The woman was found near the Bayou Sauvage National Refuge standing in waist deep water, trying to pull Broussard's body onto shore. Stay tuned for additional details.'"

I took a moment to digest the information.

"You know what's missing?"

"Yeah. The way he died."

"Exactly. If you have a suspect in custody, why not tell the public what happened? That type of information is usually only withheld if you have a flimsy case."

"But what about the twenty thousand dollars?" Brady asked.

"I can't explain away that part," I said, heading into the kitchen and grabbing the whiteboard and dry erase marker from the refrigerator. Back in the living room, Brady and I sat on the couch and went through what we knew so far.

"Let's start from the beginning. Madalyn's in jail and suspected of murdering Nathan Broussard."

"She also had a large sum of money on her," Brady added.

"Which doesn't look good, but she's stealthy and might have been doing something else with the money."

"Yes, but think about it. If this guy's wife says he's abusive and he ambushed Madalyn and the wife, I could see Madalyn snapping and protecting herself and the wife," Brady said.

"So could I, but something else could have pushed her over the edge. Another thing to consider is that the article claims she was pulling him out of the water. If she killed him, why would she do that? Why not just take off?" I scrawled a question mark on the whiteboard.

"She was set up."

"By whom?" I asked.

"The wife?"

"But Krista had turned to Madalyn for help. Speaking of which, I have read nothing about the wife."

"The spouse is usually the number one suspect, so that's a little odd, but hiring someone else to kill a husband or wife isn't exactly unheard of," Brady said.

"True. I'm going to print off the information Martin sent me about the Broussards. Once Madalyn told me this would just be a vacation, I set it aside, so I need a refresher. Maybe there's something in there we can use."

The document was only twenty pages long. I took ten pages and gave Brady the other ten. We were reading for about fifteen minutes before Brady said, "Normally, people ask if you're sitting down for shocking news, but in this instance, you need to stand."

"What's going on?" I asked.

Brady tossed the papers on to the end table.

"We need to get packed and out of here as soon as possible."

"Brady, talk to me. Why do we need to leave?"

"Nathan Broussard owns this place."

7

Brady showed me the address of the house in the middle of a long list of properties owned by Nathan Broussard.

"We're so lucky it's a holiday. Let's get out of here fast!"

"What about our fingerprints? If the police come here, they might dust for prints."

It was possible, but in the grand scheme of things, the police probably wouldn't be checking all the properties the Broussards owned for fingerprints, but better safe than sorry.

"We'll do a quick wipe down, but don't worry too much about that. The police will most likely focus on Nathan's principal residences. This is obviously a rental. Madalyn is smart enough to not talk, so they won't know she was staying here."

Brady and I packed up, wiped down the tables, doorknobs, and sink fixtures as best we could, and threw our bags in the car. I sighed and shook off the shock of discovering that we were staying on a murdered man's property.

"This thing is not looking good," Brady said as we headed to the interstate.

"No. Things are looking terrible. This makes me question everything. Madalyn was working with the wife, so I guess she could have set up these accommodations with Krista Broussard, but Madalyn had twenty thousand dollars in her pocket. None of the explanations I can come up with make that look okay."

"Sounds like a planned hit," Brady said.

"There's really no denying that. What was Madalyn doing at the bayou?"

"Didn't Madalyn say she owned this place?"

"Not exactly. I asked how long she'd had it, and she gave me a half answer. She conveniently didn't tell me it didn't belong to her."

"Not to change the subject, but where are we going?" Brady asked.

"Good question. Check for hotel vacancies. When you see something decent, let me know."

Brady scrolled through his phone while I navigated the traffic on Interstate 10.

"I found a deal. You want two rooms or one?"

"Two," I said, immediately regretting the harshness in my voice.

"I was looking at doubles, but we can go for two rooms if we need to."

"Brady, no. I'm just stressed. Book whatever you can get."

"Okay. Take exit 45. It'll be on the right-hand side of the road."

We drove the rest of the way in silence. The hotel was on the outskirts of the city in Metairie. Once we arrived, Brady went to retrieve the keys.

"I booked two rooms with an adjoining door. We'll be able to move back and forth between the two rooms with ease," Brady said, tossing a set of keys to me.

It solved an uncomfortable situation. We grabbed our bags and headed to the rooms.

"About earlier…"

"Sylvia, no need to even bring it up. Let's focus on getting Madalyn out of jail. The rest of it can wait until later."

I liked that idea. We moved our bags into our rooms and sat down in front of my laptop.

"I think we need to start with the brother and Holden Timmons, the campaign aide the reporters interviewed."

"Sounds like a good plan. Any word on the wife?"

I typed *Krista Broussard* into the search bar. A few articles came up about how she went missing after Nathan's murder.

"Well, it looks like Krista Broussard is missing. This article says she dropped off her kids at Grayson Broussard's house in the early afternoon on New Year's Eve. That's the last anyone heard from her."

"So, the wife conveniently dropped her kids off and disappeared. Sounds like the perfect setup to get rid of a husband."

"It is rather suspicious. Hopefully, this will work in Madalyn's favor. Without hearing from Nathan's wife, it's impossible to exclude her from the list of suspects."

"Sounds like reasonable doubt. Good. What about the brother and the campaign aid?"

"Grayson Broussard is a preacher," I said, typing his name into the search bar. A large structure that looked more like an auditorium than a church popped up.

"What type of church is that?" Brady asked.

"Evangelical. Pretty spiffy looking place, but it doesn't look like a church." I said, turning the computer to face Brady.

"Yeah, it puts me in the mind of a stadium," he said, moving closer to the computer screen.

I scrolled to the top of the page and viewed the schedule.

"Is church in our future? Say it ain't so," Brady asked.

"Yep. We'll be there bright and early. Unless you'd rather not go."

"I'm just thinking that it might be easier to get information if you go alone. We're not married and that might not sit well with the members."

Brady had a point. It might be easier to go alone, so we didn't have to explain anything about our relationship. Especially since I wasn't sure what was going on between us.

"Okay. Fine. The church is all me. Let's check out Holden Timmons."

I did a search for Holden Timmons, the campaign aide who'd spoken to the reporter. He was rather vocal on social media. A long tribute to his former "mentor, boss, and friend" was posted across three different platforms. The profile picture showed a baby-faced man with a crew cut and warm, brown eyes.

Brady looked over my shoulder. "Seems like that guy wants to talk about Nathan."

"Yeah. Let's give him someone to talk to. It's New Year's Day. He probably won't get back to us for a while," I said, typing out a private message asking if he would talk with me.

A message popped up almost instantly.

"Or he might be even more eager than we thought. What'd he say?" Brady asked.

"He wants to meet tomorrow at noon at Nathan's campaign office."

"It's always good to have an eager insider."

"Agreed. What have you found?"

"This is fresh off the presses. Holden must have been posting all this stuff right before he responded to your chat," Brady said, placing his phone in front of me. Holden had posted several pictures of him and Nathan. Each one was accompanied by a shot blurb paying homage to the deceased man.

"Judging from his social media, he was pretty excited about the work he was doing for Broussard," I said while Brady scrolled through Holden's previous posts.

"He posted an article about Krista Broussard being missing. The police are asking for the public's help," Brady said, showing me the article on his phone.

"Holden is quite the helper."

"It seems like he really wants to be involved, but his posts aren't getting a lot of traction," Brady said, showing me several long posts about Nathan. Each had one like.

"Who's liking the posts?" I asked.

Brady hovered his cursor over the thumbs up. "Darcy Blanchard."

"Alright. We'll keep an eye out for more interaction from Darcy. Clearly, she has a connection to Nathan, but right now, we need to find out who discovered the body, and Madalyn, in Bayou Sauvage. Then, we will look for Krista and on Sunday, I'm headed to church. You're going to regret not going," I joked.

"Whatever. So, have they published the name of the guy that came across Madalyn and Nathan's body?"

I went back to a previous list of search results and clicked on an article. "All it says is a volunteer at Bayou Sauvage found the body."

"I bet they have tons of volunteers," Brady said.

"Yeah. We'll probably just have to go there and snoop around, but we'll put that on the long list because it might take a while to find the right volunteer."

"Well, I guess we have a good place to start."

"Yeah. We'll talk with the campaign aide and the brother first, since they are not missing and we know who they are. After that, we'll try to find the wife, and the volunteer."

CARSON CALLED me that night to let me know he'd secured a lawyer for Madalyn. He sounded calm, which was vastly different from our initial conversation.

"I think she'll be out soon. The lawyer, Pascal Oliver, will meet with Madalyn tomorrow morning. He's one of the best in the state, so I don't think we have anything to worry about," Carson assured.

"Sounds good," I said, even though I felt like things were less sure than Carson made them seem. After I hung up with Carson, we raided the vending machines and made plans for the next day before heading off to bed.

WE WERE SCHEDULED to meet Holden Timmons at noon. That morning, we headed to a diner near the campaign office and the Broussard's posh neighborhood.

"Are you sure this is worth our time?" Brady asked as we climbed into the car, the morning sun shining.

"The Broussards are a prominent family. The people in the neighborhood are going to be talking about this. Also, we have to eat."

The diner was a quaint, somewhat upscale joint with an art déco design. We ordered omelets and sat quietly, listening to the surrounding conversations. A table of twenty-something men were discussing college football. The couple behind us was arguing over a potential real estate deal, and a group of women—one with pink highlights, another with wire-frame glasses pushed low on her nose, and a third with long, curly, blonde hair—were chattering about sky-high prices at the grocery store. I got up and grabbed one of the complimentary newspapers on the counter. A picture of Nathan Broussard filled the front page. I sat down and opened the paper, pretending to read it for a few minutes.

"What are you doing?" Brady whispered.

"Just watch." I sat the paper down, making sure that I perched the front page on the edge of the table.

I was sawing off a piece of my bacon and cheese omelet when the conversation turned.

"I'm not surprised Krista Broussard is missing," the woman with the glasses said.

"I know. She always had that air about herself. Nathan was friendly, but she would strut through here like she was God's gift."

"Money. She's got it all now," the woman with the glasses responded.

"Except for what she gave the killer," Pink Highlights added.

"Personally, I don't think the person they have in custody is the killer. What do you think, Jenna?"

The third woman waited for a moment before responding. Brady arched his eyebrows at me. I gave a slight nod.

"I heard Ethel Broussard is on her deathbed. Them boys are the ones that stand to benefit the most from her death, and I'm sure there was a prenup. The Broussards have held on to their money for centuries. No way they set themselves up to lose it now," Jenna said, keeping her voice low and steady.

"So, you think Grayson Broussard killed his brother for the money?" the woman with the pink highlights asked.

"No. I think Grayson's wife, Audrey, set up Krista and this person they have in custody. She's mean and greedy. My cousin went to high school with her. The Broussards are a good family, but them boys didn't pick good wives. The other one is a former beauty queen who got knocked up before the wedding. I remember how that whole thing went down. They ain't fooling no one."

"But why would Audrey go that far? The entire family has money," Pink Hair said.

"That mega-church is sucking up all the funds. Grayson is sincere, but his share of the fortune is going to be gone before he knows it. Have you seen the new church he built? Who do you think paid for that?"

"I'm sure most of it was tithes," the woman with the glasses answered.

"No, it wasn't. He don't have half the congregation to fill that place. The money came out of his pocket and Audrey hated that. She saw the writing on the wall and knew she'd better do something fast," Jenna said.

Brady and I took our time eating and squeezing in small talk while the surrounding tables cycled through different people. By the time we left, we'd learned there was a general perception that the church Grayson Broussard ran was failing because he didn't have enough charisma, and his wife was not on board with the mission.

"We'll have to find out how poorly the church is doing. Financial ruin can definitely be a motive for murder," I said, turning onto the highway.

"And if the brother's wife doesn't care for the church, she might be in the market for more money. If her husband is the only surviving offspring, there will be more for them."

"Agreed. Interesting family." I glanced at my phone. It was almost time to meet Holden. "We better hit the road. Let's see what Nathan's aide knows."

Once we were on the road, Brady said, "It sounds like Nathan was worth a lot a money, but he comes from a long line of wealth. I doubt his funds are unprotected."

"Good point. Getting the money will probably be hard and I'm sure his wife and kids will get his share."

"Unless the wife is missing and Uncle Grayson gets the kids," Brady added.

"True. Krista is still missing. Maybe she's gone for good, but

Nathan was a politician. Generally, a person in that field has a lot of enemies. I'm sure he protected his funds. We really need to find out where Krista is. She's key in all of this. If there's a prenup, that changes that game. If not, finding her might be all we need to do to save Madalyn."

8

───────────

We pulled up in front of a nondescript office building in an industrial complex. The parking lot was full of people milling around, chatting along the sidewalk, and heading to their vehicles. I spotted Holden standing out front, looking every bit as young as the pictures online had portrayed him to be. I waved to him as we parked. The slim, young man was lifting boxes into the back of a gray Dodge Ram. A man and two women stood next to Holden. We parked and headed toward the small crowd.

"Hey," the older man said, holding out his hand. "I don't recognize you two from church, but welcome, brother and sister."

"Hello," I said, taking the gentleman's hand. "Sylvia Wilcox. I'm here to talk with Holden Timmons."

"Mrs. Wilcox," Holden said, sliding another box into the truck bed. "Dad, this is the lady I told you about. Mrs. Wilcox, these are my parents, Chuck and Darla, and this here is Birdy."

"Don't be too long! We've got work to do," Birdy said, looking out over the top of her tortoise-shell glasses..

She stepped toward us. Her brow scrunched up with anger. "The real cops will be here soon! You're wasting your time,"

"Birdy, these people are trying to help. I won't be long," Holden said, turning to reassure the woman before holding out his hand.

"I appreciate you taking the time to meet with me, Holden. Sylvia Wilcox and Brady Kepler," I said, shaking hands. "And it's nice to meet all of you. Although I wish it was on better terms."

Holden gave both Brady and me handshakes. Chuck Timmons hesitated before following his son's lead and holding out his hand.

"Ms. Sylvia, I'm sorry about this. Birdy is real upset about losing Nathan. We all are, so please excuse us if we are a little off today," Holden said.

"Yeah, this is so unexpected. We're devastated," Chuck Timmons said.

"A true shock to our souls," Darla added.

"I am sorry for your loss. I hope justice is served sooner than later," I said.

"It sounds like they've got the person. No offense, but we're all kind of confused about what you're doing here," Chuck said.

I nodded. It seemed silly on the surface to be asking questions when a suspect was in custody. "I'm not a cop, but I have a drive for justice. Sometimes, the police don't have time to take a deep look at every lead. So, I lend a hand," I said.

Chuck and Darla looked at one another.

"That's B.S. You probably just snooping around to expose us as some type of hicks," Birdy said.

"C'mon ya'll. Stop this. Show some of that southern hospitality we're supposed to have," Holden said, cutting Birdy a dirty look before turning to me. "Ms. Sylvia, you see all these people leaving?"

"Yes. I noticed there was a crowd."

"Our church came by to help clean out Nathan's office. We came in this morning and started packing things up because we don't want the Broussards having to worry about such a thing at this terrible time. We're good people. You'll see that once you get to know us."

"You're right, son. Ms. Sylvia, you and your friend should stop by for dinner one of these nights," Chuck said.

"Oh yeah. I can make a roast, potatoes, and a nice peach cobbler," Darla chimed in.

"Well, ya'll better get going," Holden said.

"We'll be back later to finish cleaning. We just love the Broussards, and Pastor Grayson is so torn up about this. It's the least we can do," Darla said, reaching out and squeezing my hand.

"That's very kind of you," I said, hoping that Darla would let go of my hand soon.

"The church family is the best family," Holden said. His parents nodded and Amen-ed in agreement.

"We better go, Chuck. Pleasure to meet you two," Darla said, taking her husband's arm.

"I appreciate ya'll taking an interest in this," Holden said. He gently tugged on Birdy's long blue sweater and motioned for her to come closer.

"I'm very sorry for your loss," I said, giving Birdy a firm handshake.

She nodded. "Ya'll need coffee or anything?"

"No but thank you. Sorry about what happened to Nathan," Brady said, taking a hold of Birdy's hand. She looked over the top of her tortoise-shell glasses. Her cheeks reddened.

"Appreciate your kindness," Birdy said reluctantly letting go of Brady's hand. "I'm gonna head back in and get going on packing up more boxes."

We watched Birdy shuffle back inside the building. Holden

and Brady shared a laugh about how taken she'd been with Brady.

"What can you tell us about Nathan?" I asked, refocusing the meeting.

"He was a good man. Really into his family. I enjoyed volunteering for his campaign."

"So, you weren't technically an employee?" I asked.

"That's right. I'm still in school. My major is political science, so I started volunteering for Nathan's campaign to get some experience in the field."

"Good idea. So, you want to be a politician?"

"Kinda. But before that, I want to become a C.E.O. Just like Nathan," Holden said.

"Nice. Did Nathan have a lot of volunteers?"

"Yeah. Most are older. They have jobs and families. Me and this girl named Darcy did a lot of the work."

"Is Darcy a student as well?"

"Yep. Tulane. Just like me."

"Nice. We'd like to talk to Darcy as well. When do you graduate?" I said, shifting back to discussing Holden's life.

"Next term. Can't wait to get out in the world and do something good. Darcy is kind of shy, but I'll give you her number. I'm sure she'll want to help"

I pulled out my cellphone, opened a note, and waited for the number.

"Boy. You're ready," Holden said, a nervous giggle rippling through his body.

"I just don't want us to get to talking and forget about Darcy's number," I said, keeping my voice casual.

Holden nodded and stared off into the distance.

"I don't want anything bad to happen to Darcy."

"I totally understand. Remember, we're not police. We don't have any power to do anything. All we want is to make sure justice is done."

"Yeah, okay. That makes sense. Just don't tell Darcy I gave you her number."

"Of course, Holden. We won't say a word," I said, offering a reassuring smile.

He rattled off a number.

"Great. Thank you, Holden. So, what made you pick Nathan's campaign?"

"I attend Pastor Grayson's church. He kind of hooked me and Darcy up with the volunteer opportunity."

"I read a little about Nathan's brother. Is the church called—"

"Rise and Aspire Church, and it will change your life," Holden said, too enthusiastic to let me finish my sentence. "You need to be there to understand how powerful that place is."

"Sounds like you have a strong connection to the place," I noted.

"Oh man. That's an understatement. My life changed when I started going there. It was like a Road to Damascus kind of thing. I was sad and depressed and not sure where to go for help. One of my friends suggested Rise and Aspire and I ended up getting baptized the first day I was there."

"Must've been a powerful sermon," Brady said.

"It was. I didn't hesitate when they did the altar call. It was like a force pulled me up there and dunked me in the water. It was wonderful."

Holden's eyes had glazed over. I gave him a moment before shutting down his nostalgia and bringing him back to the conversation.

"Holden, do you know why Nathan was out at Bayou Sauvage?"

The content, distant smile disappeared from his lips.

"No. It was New Year's Eve. He told us he was leaving early, and I figured it was just for the holiday. I know he's got a wife and kids at home, so it's not my place to question the boss."

"Do you know of anyone who might want to hurt Nathan?" I asked.

"Not really. Like I said. He was a good man."

"When you say not really…"

"Okay. There were rumors, but they simply weren't true. His political opponent said Nathan was having affairs, but I know that wasn't the case, but that could have gotten someone's feathers ruffled," Holden said.

"Affairs? Anything specific? His wife, Krista, is missing."

"Nothing specific. There were just hints about affairs from the opponent. I did hear that Mrs. Broussard is missing. She's not friendly, but I think that's because the media is always following the family around. She doesn't like people photographing her kids or anything like that. At campaign rallies, she makes sure that we get plenty of shots of her and Nathan, but the kids are excluded most of the time."

"Sounds like a good mom," Brady said.

"Actually, she really is, from what I can see. Those kids are protected. A little spoiled, but safe and supported," Holden said.

"They have not found her yet, which is concerning," I said, hoping that Holden would share his thoughts on the situation.

"Hope no one went to their place and snatched her."

I waited for more. When it didn't come, I shifted back to Nathan.

"What was Nathan's political stance?"

"Politically, he was hard to pin down and some people really hated that. Was he conservative or liberal? Who knows. He just did whatever he saw fit. He liked tradition, and that's why people in this area loved him, but when it came to policy, he surprised people every now and then. That's what I respected about him."

"He wasn't partisan."

"Right. He was a lone wolf, but people kept electing him.

This time was going to be a challenge. His rival was cutting the lead in most of the preliminary polls."

It felt like Holden was trying to give me a suspect.

"What's the opponent's name?" I asked.

"Allan Gilles. Of course, due to the conservative nature of the area, Gilles wouldn't have won in the end. His politics are too liberal. It would've only gotten so close. Unless Nathan was out of the picture."

"You think it's possible Allan Gilles killed Nathan?"

Holden folded his arms and waited before responding.

"Well, it's the first thing I thought when I heard about Nathan. It'll be hard for us to build a lot of momentum for another candidate when there's no one else in the running. Nathan had been the incumbent for several terms and even though Gilles was gaining ground, I don't think he had a real chance, but now that Nathan's gone, I'm not so sure."

"There's a chance for Gilles to take the seat?"

"As crazy as it sounds, yeah," Holden said.

"You think the voters will cross party lines and vote for Gilles?"

"They will if there isn't anyone else in the running. And Gilles is sly. He knows how to say what they want to hear. He's also a successful realtor. Knows how to sell himself."

"Do you think someone else will step in?"

Holden hesitated. Clenching his jaw and squinting his eyes.

"Holden, Nathan is dead. Finding his killer is bigger than politics, and besides, I'm not from around here. Whatever you tell me stays between us," I said, fighting to keep my voice calm.

"You're right. It's just that I don't want to betray Rev's confidence."

"How would you be betraying your pastor?"

"I'm not supposed to talk about it. I know finding Nathan's killer is important, but—"

"You think the Rev is going to take up his brother's

campaign?" Brady said.

"I think the Broussards love this place. Rev will sacrifice anything to see that the parish remains a great place for families."

I took that as a *yes*.

"Did Nathan have a slogan for his campaign?"

"Keeping it Cajun."

"That resonated with his constituents?"

"Absolutely. Even if you don't have the Cajun heritage, everybody loves the culture. There have been forces around here trying to change things."

"What's Gilles' slogan?"

"Change for the better."

"Keeping things how they've been or introducing something new. Interesting dichotomy."

"Correct," Holden said. "Some of us love the way things are. Family, church, big Sunday dinners, and hanging out on the bayou. That's the way I grew up and I want my kids to have the same things. This other guy wants to dismantle our systems and change everything. Throw out faith, family, and stop being independent thinkers."

"Doesn't sound like a brilliant strategy," Brady said.

"Some people are into it. That's how this guy ended up gaining so much attention."

I saw Brady jotting down notes out of the corner of my eye.

"Did you notice Nathan acting differently in the days before his murder?"

Holden folded his arms and creased his brow.

"Not really the days before he was killed, but there was one thing that we used to talk about in the office."

"Okay. What's that?" I asked.

"Nathan let Darcy and I manage his calendar. We were under the supervision of Birdy, but Nathan wanted us to do the busy work. Sometimes, he'd pencil in appointments and they either said 'Meet Friend,' or 'Me Time.' He never told us ahead of time, so sometimes we had to cancel important appointments."

"Did you ever ask who this friend was or where he was going?"

"Yeah, but he never provided a name. He just said he had a close friend who came into town every few months and he had to make time for them."

"How long did that go on?"

Holden squinted his eyes.

"Since I've been an intern here at least, so about six months or so. Maybe more."

"Were these like lunch meetings?"

"No. Not really. He'd take a half day, sometimes a whole day, if it was a Friday."

Perfect set up for a weekend getaway.

"Any guesses who this friend was?"

"We figured it was someone from college."

"How often did Nathan take off for this friend?"

Holden scratched his head and rocked back and forth. His brow creased.

"About twice a month. I can show you his calendar."

"Great. That would be helpful. Now, was Nathan working on New Year's Eve?"

"Oddly, yes. He was making a big push right after the New Year, so we all agreed to come in and work. That day, he kept getting phone calls. There were meetings during the day, but we were constantly pausing so Nathan could step out of the office. I don't know what that was all about. They don't tell me much. I'm not real staff," Holden said.

"Can we get a look at the calendar?"

"Birdy might freak out if I tell her we're checking out Nathan's schedule," Holden said.

"Understandable, but the calendar data could be critical.

Could you take a few snapshots of a couple of months on the calendar?" I asked.

Holden diverted his eyes. "Yeah. I can do that. We'll just need to distract Birdy. She might get a little antsy if we're taking pictures of the calendar."

"Okay. Great. How should we do that?" I asked.

Holden looked at Brady. "Birdy took a liking to you. Why don't you take her up on the coffee?"

"Tons of sugar and cream?" Brady said.

"Exactly. Birdy's going to make it just right for you. While she's busy in the break room, we'll get some pictures."

"I'm always up for coffee," Brady said.

"Great. She'll make it just how you want it, so put in a few special instructions. That'll keep her busy," Holden said.

Brady headed into the office. Holden and I stood outside the door, pretending like we were talking. Birdy and Brady made small talk before he asked, in an elevated voice, "Ma'am, can I take you up on that coffee? My partner is talking with a few other people in the building. I think she'll be awhile."

"Okay. Just wait right there and I'll get you some mud. That's what we serve around here," Birdy said.

Brady pushed the door open as soon as Birdy left her desk and motioned for us to come in. Holden sprinted into the office. I followed close behind.

"Hold the pages and I'll snap pictures," Holden said.

I flipped back six months and held the pages up while Holden snapped photos of the calendar. Brady flipped through the papers on the desk.

"I don't know how this could happen to Nathan. He was such a good man," Birdy called from a room in the distance.

"I'm so sorry for your loss," Brady yelled down the hallway.

"It's so good that they caught the woman that did this. I hope they fry her. How much cream do you want?"

"Um... How about two and a half creams?"

"Two and a half... Okay. What about sugar?"

"Yeah, let's have a couple of teaspoons of sugar," Brady said.

Holden gave me a thumbs up. We slid out from behind the desk and headed back outside, carefully closing the door.

"Let me send you these," Holden said, creating a text message with the pictures of the calendar while I stuck my ear close to the door and listened to the conversation Brady was having with Birdy.

"Thanks for the coffee," Brady said. "So, I was wondering. Was Nathan's home life happy?"

"Oh yeah. He married a beauty queen, had two lovely children, and had more money than a man could ever need. Why wouldn't he be happy?"

"Sounds like the perfect life."

"It was. I grew up with his mother. She's still alive, but barely hanging on. This is going to break her. I'm so sad for her. The Broussards were dignitaries in these parts. His grandparents and great grandparents were well known and respected throughout Louisiana. It's so sad to know that someone came and took Nathan's life. His poor brother is heartbroken. Those two were so close."

"Sounds like you liked him."

"The man could do no wrong in my eyes. I hope the wife shows up soon. She's looking suspicious to me," Birdy said.

"Why do you say that?" Brady asked.

"She's not around. What does that tell you? And they found twenty thousand on the killer. That's a lot of money, and Ms. Krista would have had access to that and more."

"Interesting. So, you think Krista could have paid this woman to kill Nathan?"

"Think about it. She's gonna get a lot of money and she's five years younger than Nathan. She might have something else going on with a man from somewhere else and she ain't from around here. That might have something to do with it."

9

———

The three of us met out front of the building. I was scrolling through the pictures of the calendar as Brady peeked over our shoulders.

"I hope this helps things along. I noticed that the news hasn't reported how Nathan died. One of my professors says the cops do that when they have a weak case."

"Sometimes. In high profile deaths like this, it's risky because the public is hungry for information. I suspect they're waiting to find Krista Broussard first," I said, enlarging a picture on my phone.

"Anything interesting on the calendar?" Holden asked.

He was curious. Possibly because he was close to Nathan, but he could also be fishing for information because he knew more than he was saying.

"Nothing. I'm just seeing what we have here. Looks like Nathan was taking early days, or long weekends, about once a month."

"Sounds about right."

I looked up from my phone. Holden's eyes were wide with anticipation. He looked a little too excited for my liking.

"Thanks so much for your help. We'll be in touch," I said, giving Holden what I hoped was a warm, appreciative smile.

"Yeah, okay. Sure. Before you go, are you going to contact Darcy?"

"Yes. Thank you for her number."

"She won't know anything, but I guess you still want to talk with her."

"I do. Sometimes little things are helpful, so I like to talk with as many people that knew the victim."

Holden nodded. "Okay. I see."

Brady and I said our goodbyes and headed for the car.

"Wait," Holden called to us.

We stopped walking and turned around. "Yes, Holden?"

"There's someone else you should know about."

"Okay. Who is that?" I asked.

"Lucian Sevier."

I looked at Brady and headed back toward Holden.

"Who is Lucian Sevier?" I asked.

Holden wore a satisfied smirk. He knew I was at his mercy.

"Lucian Sevier is an oil guy from the big city. He was pushing projects that might cause problems for the seventh ward. Nathan was fighting against it. Some people were furious about it. He's having a community meeting tonight. You might want to slip in there and ask some questions."

"That sounds like a good idea. Where is this community meeting at?"

"Bethel Baptist Church. It's on Esplanade."

Brady pulled out a notepad and pen and started writing.

"Okay. What else can you tell me about Lucian Sevier?"

"Well, I think it's best if you meet Lucian and form your own opinion."

I told Holden I'd be in touch, and we headed for the car.

"Add Gilles and this Lucian man to the list of people we need to talk with," I said as we headed for the interstate.

"Done," Brady said. "So, do you think Madalyn was the friend Nathan was leaving early to see?"

"It's possible. I don't know what to think. Maybe there's more to the connection with Krista."

"But twenty thousand dollars is a decent amount of money."

"I don't feel it's enough to kill someone. Madalyn is a workhorse. She's got the yoga studio, she's a professor, and her only child is an adult. The kid earned a scholarship to college, so Madalyn should be fine financially. She wouldn't need to kill someone for money. No idea what's going on with her. I'm going to call Martin and see if he can get in touch with her daughter."

"How much contact do you have with Madalyn?" Brady asked.

"Not that much. I know she is a risk taker, hard worker, things like that. And I can always call her if I need something, but we're not really friends."

As we pulled into the hotel parking lot, Brady said, "Why did you take her up on this trip?"

"Honesty, I just really needed to get away. Life has been stressful and originally, this was going to be a work trip. Once Madalyn called everything off and said she still wanted to take a trip, I decided it was a good idea. All I was doing at home was... being lonely. I was sad and just looking for a way to break out of my funk."

"Understandable. What if you find out that Madalyn is the killer?"

"She's not."

"We were staying in one of Nathan Broussard's residences, but Madalyn pretended like it was hers. She could be hiding other things."

It was a good point. There was no telling what was really going on with Madelyn. She wasn't the most honest person I knew, but I couldn't just leave her in jail in Louisiana. There was no way she'd killed Nathan Broussard. Right?

BACK AT THE HOTEL, I looked for information about Allan Gilles. His campaign website was flashy. Loud, upbeat music played the moment you clicked on the site, and a video of an extremely tall man with dark skin, elongated eyelashes, and a bit of mascara walked into the scene. A tiny Asian woman and two children entered the frame from the other side.

"Life in our beautiful state is good, but it's not as good as it could be. We need to make a change, ladies and gentlemen. Come out and vote for change. I'm different and I plan to create a unique experience for all of us. Not just certain groups." The music kicked back up before the video ended.

"What's his platform?" Brady asked.

"Being different, I suppose." I scrolled down to the bottom of the page. "His office is a few miles up the road. I think we should stop by."

"Now?"

"No time like the present," I said, grabbing the car keys.

Allan Gilles's office was in Metarie, in a strip mall squeezed into the corner of the complex. It was only about 400 square feet, but campaign signs and stickers covered the door. Before I could ring the bell, a man wearing just the slightest hint of eyeliner opened the door.

"May I help you?" Allan Gilles asked.

I held out my hand. "I'm Sylvia Wilcox, and this is Brady Kepler. We're looking into Nathan Broussard's murder. Are you Mr. Allan Gilles?"

"Yep. Come on in. It's small, but it was all I needed," he said, providing an unneeded explanation.

The office was neat and organized. A pile of flyers sat on the desk next to a phone, and a small woman wearing a blue sundress was at the filing cabinet. Two children, younger than five, were playing with Legos in the far corner of the room.

"This is my family," he said. "Rhea, my wife, my daughter, Angel, and my son, Ryan."

Brady and I greeted the family, shaking hands with his wife.

"I'll take the kids outside," Rhea said.

Allan Gilles smiled and nodded.

"I feel honored that I'm relevant enough for you to come and talk to me. The police haven't stopped by yet," he said, his eyebrows lifting high on his head.

"Interesting. Well, I'm happy that you agreed to talk to me. I'm curious about the campaign."

"A needed change. Things have been great around here for all the Cajun folks, but those of us that don't fit into that box haven't been having as much fun. I wanted to make things more even around here, but at no point did I want Nathan dead. I wanted to beat him fair and square."

"I heard the polling was close."

"Never so close that I was going to win. Maybe in a few years, but the area I'm running for is still pretty Cajun. So, no ma'am. I wouldn't hurt Nathan. He's gone now and I'm still not going to win."

Gilles seemed rather settled on the fact that he would not win. He seemed nonchalant about the situation.

"I think the brother is going to get into the race and he will go after my lifestyle. People will buy it too, but that's okay. I never expected to win."

"Is that still the plan? To lose?"

"Yeah. Grayson has this in the bag. Everyone knows it."

"Then why are you running?"

"Think of me as the impetus to change. Eventually, the

dynasty will lose its grip and people will vote for something different."

"A sacrifice."

"Something like that. So, killing Nathan Broussard would be silly. If it's not him, it'll be his brother. This wasn't a true fight for power. It's more of a fight to be recognized. But that's enough about me. Here's the thing. If you two are looking for a suspect, check out that big oil honcho. Nathan and I agreed on the environmental stuff. This dude, Lucian, had a scandalous plan that would put all the waterways at risk. He wanted to drill a ton of wells in our lakes. The sad part is that Grayson is all for it, because it's money and he's nothing like Nathan."

"He doesn't care about the environment?" Brady asked.

"That's an understatement. If something makes money, he's for it. That's why he's running a church. And here's the thing. I couldn't find dirt on Nathan. Squeaky clean. Grayson is the prodigal son mixed with Cain. Just dig deeper than what the newspapers printed back in the day, and you'll find all you need," Allan said.

"Thanks for the tip. We'll look for information on unofficial channels. Is there anything else you can tell us about Nathan? His wife is missing."

"Oh yeah. Miss Thang is missing, so that's something. She is a diva that doesn't like to be bothered. Not mean, but not nice and too closed off to be a politician's wife."

"No rumors of mistresses or anything like that?" Brady asked.

Allan smiled. "Someone tried to say that I started rumors about Nathan having affairs, but I didn't. There's no way anyone in their right mind would believe that. He was all about family and community, but only his community. Not because he was a bad guy. He's just like the rest of us. We protect our own, right?"

Brady and I both nodded.

"But I don't think the diva would murder anyone. Did Grayson pay someone to kill his brother? That's possible. And the killer had twenty thousand dollars on her. That's chump change for a Broussard."

10

We finished up with Allan Gilles and headed back to the hotel.

That afternoon, I called Martin and asked him to get a hold of Madalyn's daughter. I hoped she would be able to let Martin into Madalyn's office to get a peek at her calendar.

"Looks like the community meeting starts at five," Brady said once I was off the phone.

"Great. We should probably head there now."

The church was small and cozy without adornments or much beside pews. The community hall had several rows of chairs set up and the place was already packed when we showed up. Small groups debated about a pipeline that would run close to neighborhoods. Crabmen, fishermen, and residents that loved the water were represented based on the snippets of conversation we picked up. At five sharp, the crowd went silent, and the pastor headed to the front.

"Brothers and sisters, we're pleased to have Mr. Lucian Sevier here to tell us what plans he'd like to see happen here in our neighborhood. Now, let him speak and be respectful."

The pastor put the microphone down and took a seat. A tall, thin man dressed in an expensive black suit walked from the back of the room, taking long strides. He wasn't traditionally attractive, but there was something alluring about him. I watched him move to the crowd with sleek, graceful movements, almost like a cat, a crooked smirk forming on his lips. People in the crowds called out to him while others clapped.

"Good people of the magnificent seventh ward of the great city of New Orleans. My name is Lucian Sevier and I'm here to say, let's come together to build a better future. We will bring this place back, but the only way that we do that is with industry. We have the greatest industry there is for this area. We will invest millions of dollars into New Orleans East and bring this part of the city back better than it was before. Let us help you." Lucian spread his hands in front of them, sleek and poised.

The room fell silent and remained the way for most of Lucian Sevier's speech. Lucian spent the next half an hour laying out a plan that would bring jobs and money to the area. At the end of the talk, Lucian opened the floor to questions and allowed residents to come up and talk with him.

People gathered near him laughing, smiling, wanting to be in his presence. It was strange. He was wearing a perfectly pressed black suit and as he walked carefully to the crowd of people, people got it to hear him speak. Lucian was tall, much taller than everybody else in the room.

"This guy knows how to work a room," Brady said.

"This guy knows how to work a room," Brady said.

"He certainly knows how to do that," I replied. "I've got a few questions for him. Let's get closer."

Brady and I made our way to the front of the stage, carefully inching towards Lucian. He was shaking hands and joking with a group of people.

"I want to know what the plan is for New Orleans East. Why are you so interested in that part of town?" I asked.

Lucian turned around and took my hand.

"It is nice to meet you. Whom do I have the pleasure of speaking with?" Lucian asked, sticking his hand out.

"I'm a concerned citizen."

"Folks, let me speak with this dear woman. Just give me a minute." Lucian said, putting a cold hand on my back and gently leading me towards an empty corner of the room.

"Why can't we talk amongst the crowd?" I asked.

Lucian smiled. "I don't know why you're here, but I recommend you go back to your little Yankee paradise up north. These people don't need you down here interfering with their lives. You look milk fed and if you're able to spend endless time away from home, I'm guessing you've got a little money. Not as much as me, but some money. That means you don't need to be here trying to fix all the world's problems. So what is it you want, ma'am?"

"I'm just curious about how this new project is going to help the average person in this area."

"Okay. I'm going to need a little personal time with this one, folks," Lucian said to the crowd before gently slipping a hand behind my back and leading me to an empty corner of the room.

"Consider us an old company that cares. We see the inequality in this state and we're looking to make a difference. What's your name ma'am? You know mine. It's only fair that I know yours."

"Sylvia."

"Okay, well Ms. Sylvia. Let's talk about this. Our company is trying make life better for people. Isn't that what makes the world special? People like me who make a difference? Have you been there at night, Ms. Sylvia? Have you spent evenings at barbecues in a deepest, darkest ghettos, or been to one of the tiny Vietnamese restaurants that are run out of little nooks and crannies? Are you a part of all of this? Or are you just another outsider laughing at these people and all their poverty and superstitions?"

Lucian was standing a few inches in front of me. His face was close enough for me to smell the hint of leftover menthol mouthwash. He stared deep into my eyes, causing a shiver to run through my body. He raised a hand to my cheek. A cold, clammy, rough hand slid along the side of my face.

"Ms. Sylvia, you don't know what you're getting yourself into. I suggest you back off and go home to that big ole Victorian that your dead husband bought you. Fix up that fourth bathroom in the basement, maybe get the kitchen redone, and get rid of the big pine table you have. Get something more suitable. Maybe something for one," Lucian said, his bottom lip touching the tip of my nose.

I pulled away. How could he possibly know anything about my life? How did he know I lived in an old Victorian? I was breathing hard, and I wanted to leave, but it felt like my body was frozen in place. Lucian smiled, his lips curling into an evil smirk. How did he know about my house? Knowing that I owned an old Victorian wouldn't have been shocking if he'd met me before. A simple search would turn that information up, but I'd only just met him. Also, how did he know I had a huge pine table? A shiver ran through my body. *The devil's greatest trick is convincing us he doesn't exist.* I shook off the thought.

"Sylvia?" Brady said, gently grabbing my arm. "Are you ready to go?"

I turned to face Brady. It felt like I had control over my body as soon as I broke eye contact with Lucian.

"Yes. I think we're done here."

"SOMETHING IS WRONG WITH HIM," I said as I buckled my seatbelt.

"Yeah, he's a suit on a mission. There's always something wrong with those guys."

"No. It was something more. I felt like I couldn't move when I was talking to him, and he knew things he couldn't possibly know... Unless..."

"Unless what?"

"I don't know. I feel so out of sorts."

"Okay. Let's run through our persons of interest," I said, motioning for Brady to follow me into my room. As soon as we were inside, I noticed my laptop was open on the bed. I always closed my computer, and it was on the table when I left that morning. I was sure of it.

"Did you move my computer before we left?"

Brady shrugged. "No. I haven't touched it. Why?"

"I didn't leave it on the bed."

"You probably just forgot. Come on, let's go over our suspects," Brady said, gently tugging at my arm.

"Wait. I want to call Darcy." I punched her phone number into my phone and listened to two rings before the call was sent to voicemail. *You know who you called. Leave me a message.* A soft voice with a heavy southern accent purred into the phone. I left my number and asked Darcy to return my call, without explaining why I was calling.

"Okay," I said. "Suspects. Who do we have?"

"The wife. She's missing. Either because she's a victim too, or she orchestrated the whole thing."

"Yeah, the fact that she hasn't turned up is very suspicious." I said, writing Krista's name on the board.

"Allan Gilles?"

"Unlikely, but maybe. We'll keep him on the list for now."

"The brother."

"More likely," I said. "We'll need to get in touch with him."

"And it sounds like everyone thinks this Lucian person is bad news."

"True. Let's discuss the other suspects. Then, we'll look into Lucian. But... we also have to add Madalyn to the list."

"Are you sure?"

"She was in contact with Nathan. Madalyn claimed she was helping the wife, but there was also a connection with Nathan. What was going on there?"

"No idea. It is very weird."

"The twenty thousand really bothers me. Who gave Madalyn the money?"

"The brother is making comments to the media, and the wife is missing. Either one could be seen as suspicious on the surface, but the money could have come from someone else entirely."

"What if things got screwed up? What if neither the wife nor the brother gave Madalyn the money? Maybe the husband was there and there was a struggle. What if Nathan showed up to kill his wife and Madalyn killed him in self-defense?"

"Madalyn isn't known to hurt estranged husbands."

"Do we really know that?"

"Well, as far as I know, Madalyn doesn't hurt the husbands. Her operation is clandestine, but she's sincere. I think if Nathan was getting violent with Krista, she may have killed him," I said.

"But wouldn't she have admitted it? That's self-defense," Brady said.

"Yeah. Madalyn's honest to a point, but something happened there. She may have showed up, and the husband was already in the bayou, dead. Why was he there, and where is the wife?"

"Krista needs to turn up soon."

"Well, she's apparently a diva of some sort, but what if she's betting that everyone thinks that about her?"

"What are you getting at?" I asked.

"Think about it. If she's got this image of being upper crust or whatever, hiding out in the slums would keep her out of sight. Everyone will look in fancy hotels and things like that."

"Brady, that's a good idea. Let's check out the properties. See if any of them are in dangerous neighborhoods."

I pulled the stack of papers with the Broussard properties on them out of my computer bag, found the pages with property listings, and split them in half.

"Let's see how many of these places are occupied."

We combed through the addresses, searching for each property online. Three properties were in less than desirable areas, and several others were unoccupied. I jotted down the addresses on a notepad.

"Tomorrow I'll head to the church in the morning. Will you research the properties? Narrow them down and see if any stand out as good places to hide out."

"Yes, ma'am," Brady said, saluting me.

"Great. Let's get dinner and call it a day."

THE NEXT MORNING, I was on the road by eight, en route to Rise and Aspire Church. I'd left Brady at the hotel. He was separating the Broussard properties into occupied and unoccupied when I left. We planned on checking the ones in seedy areas to see if Krista had taken refuge in any of them.

I pulled into the church's parking lot half an hour before the first service. The church was tucked in-between the city, several empty fields, and an island urban sprawl. The building looked like a small stadium, with few clues to what type of business was practiced there. Several other smaller structures lined the campus, but for all its enormity, only a few cars were in the parking lot. I'd showed up half an hour early, hoping that there'd be a few people around I could talk with. The doors slid open, and I stepped into a large café space. There still weren't any religious images to show this was a church. I knew Grayson had invested in the building, so he wasn't renting the space. It was an odd choice for a house of worship.

I headed for a long string of doors that led into an auditorium. A woman with large, red rimmed glasses pushed down on her nose was walking around placing programs at the end of each row of seats.

"Hello," I said, walking down the main aisle.

"Service starts in half an hour," the woman responded without looking up.

"Oh, thank you," I said. "Would you mind if I asked a few questions? I'm looking for a new church home."

The woman stopped placing flyers on the seats and looked up. Telling religious people you're interested in their faith is the best way to get their attention.

"What would you like to know?"

"What are the rules about joining? Do you have to volunteer or tithe? I'm working two jobs trying to catch up on some bills and don't have much money."

"Giving ten percent of your income is a requirement of the bible. If you feel like you can't do that, you can volunteer to clean the church or run errands for Pastor Grayson."

"Okay. Is this a bible-based church or are there additional beliefs?"

"Faith alone. What else would you need? We believe every word in the bible, which is the word of the Lord."

Every word? I wondered if she was only talking about the New Testament. I nodded my head.

The woman said, "If you joined the church, young lady, you will have a meeting with Pastor Grayson and he will decide the right path for you."

"The right path?"

"Yeah. Pastor Grayson guides us on our path to salvation.

He's an amazing man," the woman said, her eyes wide with admiration.

"How long have you been a member?"

"Only six months. I was at the end of my rope. One Sunday, I was crying, and I wanted someone to hold me. I wandered the streets, and I heard a woman singing *Amazing Grace*. It was beautiful. I felt like I was in a daze, and something carried me into the church. It was this mystical experience."

The woman's eyes had clouded over. I let her stare at the far wall of the church for a few more second before saying, "That's a great story."

The woman reached out for my hand, similar to the way Darla Timmons had done the day before at Nathan Broussard's office.

"It is like nothing I've ever experienced. I want that for you."

The woman peered into my eyes. I diverted my gaze to the floor. This was so uncomfortable.

"Sounds great," I said, gently pulling my hand away from hers.

Her eyebrows creased as if she'd just been pulled out of a trance. I wasn't sure what to do, so I pushed my hand back toward her for a shake.

"Oh. Yeah, I'm Jade. Nice to meet you."

"Same. Sounds like this is a good place to be," I said. Careful to leave my name up to chance.

"It is."

"What can you tell me about Pastor Grayson?"

"He's a great guy. Kind of like a prophet. His family is great. Audrey, his wife, runs the women's group, his teenagers lead youth activities, and you can see how deep their faith runs."

"That's good to hear. I don't want to be involved in any church that's going to run into scandal. I need the real deal."

Jade tilted her head.

"You're asking because you've heard about Nathan."

I folded my arms and wrinkled my brow. "I just want to make sure I'm getting involved with good people. I've had some bad experiences with churches."

"I can see that. You feel injured. I'm an empath. I feel so much. Sit down," Jade said, gently touching my arm.

"What happened to Pastor Grayson's brother?"

Jade reached over and grabbed my hand.

"Men are fallible. I don't like to gossip, but it's just one of those things where there's one good brother and one bad one. Like Cain and Abel. Nathan was very secular. He didn't always make it to church, and he had dealings with all types of people. Not just good Christian folks."

I bit my tongue and thought of a proper response.

"Nathan wasn't religious?"

"Not religious enough. You see what's happened to him. Dead and his wife is missing. That family needed an anointing, and it just didn't happen soon enough."

"Was Pastor Grayson close to his brother?" I asked.

"You've probably heard that he was a member here. That's true, but Grayson kept him in order. As a politician, Nathan carried a certain presence, but it was clear he wasn't the good brother."

"Why is that?"

"His wife looked so unhappy. But that's enough of that bad talk. Stick around for service. You'll see things are different here."

Jade touched my arm before heading off to continue placing programs at the end of each row. I headed back into the foyer. People were arriving, and I didn't want to run into Holden, so I headed upstairs to the second level.

The first service began at nine. I stayed out in the concourse and watched people enter the sanctuary. The crowd was decent, but the church was too big for the number of members.

Once the service began, I headed to a seat at the top of the second level. The lights dimmed, and a band played a melody. As Grayson Broussard emerged on the stage, applause filled the building.

"The Lord will not let you down, my friends," Grayson yelled into his headset. The crowd went wild.

Grayson was a little over six feet with a neat crew cut, a perfect smile, and a crisp, pressed, dark blue suit. His features were chiseled and attractive and every hair on his head was carefully sculpted.

"God bless you. Welcome to Glory!" Grayson said, stringing together random phrases.

"My brother did all he could to make this place better. And the goal, my friends, is to be able to tell St. Peter that we did all we could to improve the world while we were on this planet. When you get to the pearly gates, you need to have a good story to share with St. Peter, and if you don't, you run the risk of being struck down and sent to the fiery pit!"

Again, the crowd yelped and screamed in adulation. I was in the back of the top row of the stadium like sanctuary. Looking down onto the first level, the people looked like ants. I moved close to the balcony edge, clapping and scanning the crowd. I spotted Holden, Darla, and Chuck cheering. A young woman with shoulder-length brown hair was standing next to Holden. She was clapping, but from where I was standing, I could see that the young woman wasn't as enthused as the Timmons family.

"I can't hear you," Grayson said, sticking his hand to his ear. I'd seen a similar move during professional wrestling matches. The thump of the crowd was overwhelming, like we were at a concert.

"The demons will try to stop us, but we won't let them. Nathan was fighting demons and I will not let his legacy be forgotten. I said a prayer this morning, and I asked for direction. I wanted to know what the good Lord wanted me to do to honor my brother, and he told me there is only one way."

Grayson stopped for effect. The crowd fell silent, waiting in great anticipation.

"Friends, I am going to step into Nathan's shoes and even though I can never fill them, I will do my best to make the good Lord happy."

Another roar rang out. The sounds were deafening. I'd seen enough. I quietly slipped out of the sanctuary and headed for the car.

Nathan had only been dead a few days. Announcing that he was going to slip into his brother's shoes was disturbing. Grayson Broussard moved to the top of the suspect list.

11

—————

"How was church?" Brady asked without looking up from the computer.

"Loud and interesting. Grayson Broussard is going to pick up where Nathan left off and run for senate."

"Really? Wow! I guess that's part of his grieving process."

"Exactly. I also think I saw Darcy there with Holden."

"Yeah? Did you talk to her?"

"Nope. I stayed off in the distance. She looked less than enthused than the Timmons family about the sermon."

"Did you get a chance to talk with Grayson?" Brady asked.

"No. I just wanted to get out of there. I was uncomfortable there."

"Okay, well I've been looking at places I think Krista might be. It looks like there are three properties that aren't occupied. The rest are rented."

"Where are these places located?"

"One in the 9th ward, one in the 2nd, and one in the 17th."

Brady handed me a small map.

"We're pretty close to the 17th. Why don't we head there now?"

"Sounds like a plan."

The 17th ward encompasses a stretch of land that goes from the Mississippi to Lake Pontchartrain. The property was a duplex that looked like it hadn't been lived in for years. Both doors were boarded up, but the yard was cut.

"I read that part of the city suffered during Katrina," Brady said. "It looks like the Broussards had a couple of properties in areas like that. I figure no one would look here."

"You're right. It's pretty run down."

The neighborhood was not empty, but there were clear signs that the hurricane had caused massive flooding in the area. Houses, likely built in the wake of World War II, were battered and strung together with random pieces of corrugated steel. Weaved in between the dilapidated houses were well kept brick homes, which probably were older than the houses that were falling down. We parked in front of the duplex.

"This is pretty sketchy," Brady said.

"Agreed. I've got my gun. Stay close and we'll be fine."

My heartbeat quickened as I opened the car. I felt out of my element. The street was empty except for a tall man, too far away for me to see his face. He took long, powerful strides, but it seemed like he wasn't getting any closer. His skin was pale and his hair thick and black. He was dressed head to toe in a dark suit. I stared down the street. Something was off.

"Sylvia, you okay?" Brady asked.

"Yeah. I just..." I looked at Brady for a moment and then again down the street. The man was gone. Sweat had formed on my forehead and my heart still thumped against my chest.

"Why don't you get back in the car? I can go look around," Brady said.

"No. Let's go." I closed the door and looked down the street again. No one was there. I shook off the thought. Maybe no one had been there in the first place.

"Let's get this over with," Brady said.

"Yep. Let's do this."

We walked over to the house. Since the front doors were boarded up, we split up and looked in the windows on each side of the house. The windows all had bars, which were covered in cobwebs. I peered into the house. Pipes, food wrappers, and old furniture were present, but it didn't look like there were any active squatters, including Krista.

"Looks pretty insignificant from what I can see," Brady said.

"Same here. I don't think Krista has been here."

"Time to head out?"

"You got it. Let's roll."

"Looks like it's been vacant for a while. Hurricane Katrina really messed things up around here. Seems like this place has never been the same," Brady said as we climbed into the car.

"Did you see a guy down the street? Tall, dressed in black. Giving off a vampire vibe? Kind of looked like Lucian Sevier?"

Brady laughed. "Um... No. What are you talking about?"

"Nothing. I just thought I saw something. Probably just tired. Anyway, where are the other houses?"

"One in the 2nd and one in the 7th."

"Let's head to the 2nd. We'll save the 7th for tomorrow morning. I want to check out Bayou Sauvage. It's located there, so we'll head over before going to the bayou."

Brady's phone provided robotic instructions to the house. It was in much better shape than the previous property. Painted in bright yellow and pink tones, it was clear work had recently been completed.

"They probably were going to rent this one soon," Brady said.

"I think you're right. Looks good."

We poked around a bit, but no one had been living in the house for a while.

"I don't think she's been here," I said. "Back to square one."

FRUSTRATED, we headed back to the hotel. As soon as I pushed open the door to my room, I knew something was wrong. The papers with the Broussard's addresses were on the floor near the bed.

"What's wrong?" Brady asked.

I stood frozen in the doorway. Had someone been in my room? Maybe the maid had been by? But she didn't come that early in the day and if she had, why hadn't anything been cleaned? The bed was still unmade and the trash hadn't been emptied.

"The papers were on the bed when we left."

Brady shrugged. "They must have slipped off."

"The bed is flat and none of the windows are open."

"Yeah," Brady said, nonchalant.

I stepped through the doorway, looking around to see if anything else was out of place.

"You okay?"

"Yeah. I'm just checking to see if things are where I left them," I said.

While I was looking underneath the bed, Martin called. I abandoned my search and answered the phone, but I was sure someone had been in my room.

"I got a hold of Madalyn's schedule. Carson let me into her place last night. What I found was really interesting."

"Hold on. Let me put you on speaker so Brady can hear too." I sat my phone on the nightstand and turned on the speakerphone.

"Madalyn traveled to Louisiana on the following dates: March 1st, April 15th, May 27th, July 2nd, September 2nd, and November 22nd."

I wrote down the dates and repeated them back to Martin.

"Some of the dates are close to holidays," Martin said. "Memorial Day, 4th of July, Labor Day, and Thanksgiving."

"The other dates are Fat Tuesday and Good Friday. Big days here in New Orleans."

"So, were these trips business or pleasure?"

"It's hard to say. Let me check the snapshots from Nathan's calendar. Nathan had taken Fat Tuesday and Good Friday off— days a person would probably take off if they lived here. The rest of the holidays were ones that any politician would have off, so that's not really a sign that Nathan and Madalyn were together. In fact, the days Nathan left early and wrote, 'Friend from out of town' don't line up with the dates Madalyn traveled here."

"So, we're off base with this," Martin said.

"Yeah, it's not the smoking gun I'd hoped it would be. Madalyn isn't religious, and she tends to not care about holidays, but those are good times to come here and help get women out of abusive situations."

"Maybe she also met with the wife while she was there. What have you and Brady discovered?"

"Hold on. Let me get Brady on so we can all talk," I said, switching my phone to speaker mode.

"Not much. We really need to talk to Krista. It's strange that she's still MIA."

"If Krista is dead, then unfortunately, I think we have to except that Madalyn might be the perpetrator.

"Come on, we've worked with her before. She's not that type of woman," Brady said.

"We need more information. Martin, check online for reviews or any information you can find about Madalyn's yoga studio, or her as a professor, and see if you can track down her daughter, Kara. It seems like something has changed for Madalyn."

"You really think she killed this guy? C'mon Sylvia. There's no way. You can't believe she's the killer," Martin said.

"No, but she had twenty thousand dollars on her when she was arrested. We can't ignore that. Why did Madalyn have that money on her?"

12

My phone rang around six the next morning.

"Yes, I'm looking for a Ms. Sylvia Wilcox." The man on the other end had a slow and steady drawl.

It took a moment for the words to register before I said, "Yes. You have her. How can I help you?"

"My name is Paschal Oliver and I'm representing Ms. Madalyn Price. Mr. Carson Stark gave me your number. I really need to meet as soon as possible. We've got a situation."

"Is Madalyn alright?" I asked, snapping to awareness and fearing the worst.

"Well, she's in jail and facing a possible murder charge, but she's okay. There's something we need to discuss. It's not really phone talk, so can we meet? I can come to you if that helps."

"No. We'll meet you somewhere. Name the place."

"We?"

"Me and.... Listen, that's complicated. Just name a place and we'll be there soon. Someone... a guy named Brady is helping me look into things, and he'll be with me."

"Is this your assistant?"

"No. My assistant's back in Michigan."

Paschal was quiet for a moment before saying, "I knew I shouldn't have taken this case."

"Meet me at Anderson's Cafe in town," I said.

"Fine. See you in half an hour."

"Sounds good."

I hung up and headed straight for the shower. After throwing on a pair of black pants and a cream-colored top, I headed for the adjoining doors that separated my room from Brady's.

"Hey, are you up?" I asked through the door.

"Yeah. Come on in."

Brady was already dressed. It looked like he'd been up for hours.

"What are you doing?"

"Couldn't sleep last night, so I got up around five, went for a walk, and headed to the lobby. Got us some breakfast stuff," he said, pointing to a spread of fruits and pastries.

"That's so nice. Thank you," I said, heading over and grabbing an apple.

"What's going on?"

"Madalyn's lawyer just called. We need to meet with him in half an hour."

"Okay. I'll make this quick. I've been thinking. Why would Madalyn be with Nathan? She was working with the wife who said she was being abused. That doesn't make sense."

"I know. I don't get it at all."

"I have a theory," Brady said.

"I'm all ears."

"What if both Madalyn and Nathan were connected in some way that wasn't related to Krista?"

"Like they were friends, or... Maybe they worked together?" I said, setting down the apple I had in my hand.

"Yeah. Think about it. Nathan seems to have been a humanitarian. So is Madalyn. It's not unreasonable to think that they may have worked on something together." Brady said.

"Madalyn was traveling here often and while the dates don't line up perfectly, she was around when Nathan would take off from the office, saying he was meeting a friend."

"Which could have been code for we're going to save someone from an unpleasant situation. It seems like that was a mutually important thing to them." Brady folded his arms and creased his brow.

"I hadn't thought of it in those terms, but Madalyn would be open to helping. I'm sure of that. Good job, Brady. We'll explore this later. Let's hit the road."

The Monday morning traffic was moderate but we were able to get across town in about fifteen minutes. We found a parking space a few houses down from the restaurant and headed for the restaurant.

Anderson's was an eclectic, beautiful house on the west side of the side. Nestled in a neighborhood of houses painted bright, vibrant colors. A tall, heavyset man in a dark blue suit in front of an orange house.

"Mr. Oliver?" I asked as we walked toward the man.

The lawyer was clean cut, with short brown hair and dark piercing eyes. He was tall and heavyset, and he looked a little uncomfortable in the expensive suit he was wearing.

"Sylvia Wilcox," I said, holding out my hand.

Paschal smiled and shook my hand. He cast a sly smirk at Brady.

"This is Brady," I said, not knowing exactly how to introduce him. Was he my sidekick? Just a friend? Something more?

"Nice to meet both of you." Paschal arched his eyebrows at me. He looked like a Cheshire cat.

"Ms. Sylvia, I hope you can help me with some answers because we've got a real barn burner," he said in a slow Texas drawl.

"Let me guess, Madalyn is being uncooperative?"

"To say the least. She told the story, but nothing's shaking out. I really hope you can help."

"We'll try."

"Ya'll hungry?"

I looked at Brady. He shook his head.

"Not really. Maybe we can just grab coffees?"

"Yeah. Let's do that," Paschal said. A row of tables was set up in front of Anderson's.

We sat at a four top near the sidewalk. A painfully thin woman with long red hair came up to the table and took our order. Brady and I had black coffee, but Paschal ordered some type of fancy mocha and a beignet.

"Okay. How can we help?" I asked after the server walked away.

"Well, Madalyn told me she's got some charges back in Michigan that might affect her getting bail."

I shook my head. "Um, Madalyn Price? What charges? Are you sure that's what she said?"

"Apparently, she got into some trouble back home. Do you know anything about that?"

"Not in the slightest. I know she's a college professor and a yoga teacher. I don't know what type of trouble she would be in, but it seems like that kind of trouble might affect her work."

"Well, according to her, she's just a yoga instructor," Paschal said.

"Really?"

"Yeah. She told me she's put the professorship and the counseling on hold. Do you know when that happened?"

"Not at all. I guess I should explain. Madalyn and I are associates, but she's very secretive. We've worked together in the past and I know a little about her background, but her day-to-day life is a mystery to me," I said.

"Oh. Well, she told me it's been about a year for both. But it would be good to know the details. I took the liberty to call up north and get information."

It'd been years since I looked into Madalyn Price. Back when she was a suspect years ago, her background had been squeaky clean, besides her covert rescue operation for women and children.

"What type of charges are we talking about?"

"There was something to do with a domestic disturbance."

"Do you know who filed the charges?"

"Ironically, Carson Stark is the person that pressed charges against Madelyn."

"Wait a minute," Brady interjected. "Madalyn beat up the dude that hired you?"

"That's what it sounds like. He's paying me to be her lawyer while simultaneously pressing charges against her. I've never seen anything like this before."

"I can't believe that," I said.

"Madalyn hasn't explained it to me and I'm hoping you can shine some light on the situation. I will call Mr. Stark and ask, but since he neglected to mention it, I figure he doesn't want to talk about it."

"It sounds like there's more to Carson and Madelyn's relationship than meets the eye," Brady said.

"That right. And just like you two have some type of history you're not willing to explain, Mr. Stark and Madalyn Price seem to be in the same boat. The difference is that I have to know what's going on between the two."

"Understandable. I'll see what I can find out," I said.

"My time doesn't come cheap, and I have a family back home. I would appreciate any help," Paschal said.

I felt lost. Madalyn had asked me to call Carson, and he'd hired a lawyer immediately. But they'd had some type of domestic dispute. Was it something to do with the kids? I did not know, but something more was going on.

"Carson and Madalyn have an interesting connection. Madelyn's daughter is the half-sister of Carson's stepdaughter. Carson officially adopted his stepdaughter after his wife was murdered. There are also two younger kids from Carson and his wife. The two younger ones are half siblings of Danica, who is also Madalyn's daughter's half-sister. If Carson and Madalyn were getting together, it could have gotten messy."

"Perhaps there was some type of feud that involved the kids?" Brady said.

"Okay. Slow down here. So, Madalyn's daughter... What's her name?" Paschal asked.

"Kara."

Paschal pulled out a notepad and jotted down the name.

"She's the half-sister to Mr. Stark's stepdaughter?"

"Correct."

"Who is Madalyn's daughter's father? I assume she shares a father with Mr. Stark's stepdaughter," Paschal said.

"Yes. He's in prison. Not a nice guy or someone either girl was in contact with last I heard."

"I don't know, but I feel like my client and the man that hired me are not telling me the full story."

"I have to agree," I said, wondering what could've happened between Carson and Madalyn.

"This is a death penalty state and the person that's dead is cherished in these parts. No jury is going to take it easy on her," Paschal explained.

"I understand. We'll gather some information and see if we can help piece together what's going on."

"Don't take too long. Clock's a ticking."

13

———

"This keeps getting weirder. Do you think Madalyn will get bail? I think there's a lot she needs to clear up if we're going to help her," Brady said as we climbed back into the car.

"So, Carson and Madalyn had a fight of some sort. Maybe this is also tied in with Nathan," Brady said.

"This angle makes sense. If Madalyn was having a relationship with Carson, but also traveling a lot, it could have caused problems for them."

"Absolutely. The excessive travel probably didn't go over well. I wonder how Nathan's wife fits into all of this?"

"Me too. Let's get back to our hunt for Krista," I said. "You remember where the next house is located?"

"Kind of. Let me pull it up."

We stared at Brady's phone. The Broussard property was a small, run-down, clapboard, blue house.

"This place looks like it hasn't been occupied in some time," I said.

"Might be the perfect hiding place, and it is right by where Nathan was found. Let's check it out," Brady said, grabbing the car keys.

We took the I-10 back to the 7th ward. I pulled up the directions on my phone and helped Brady navigate the city streets. While we drove, Brady told me about the area.

"After Hurricane Katrina, some people didn't return to the city, and some continued to live in FEMA trailers. Certain sections of the city have never come back. The 7th isn't as bad as the 9th, but things are still bad and it's a high crime area."

The neighborhood was quiet and still. Some houses appeared to be occupied, while others were completely boarded up. Brightly colored duplexes lined the street, weaved in between single-family homes.

We parked around the corner and headed to the address in the middle of the block. The sun beat down upon us as we walked toward the house. The air was thick and humid, and an eerie silence greeted us. Overgrown fields, burned-out cars, and boarded-up houses created the perfect environment for crime.

"We need to be careful," I told Brady.

We walked towards the middle of the block, approaching a blue house.

"Hey, I think I read something about blue houses here. Something about protection," Brady said.

I nodded. "Yeah. It's called Haunt Blue. I remember hearing stories about the color blue being protective. I guess this house could be the perfect place to hide if you believe in that type of thing."

I paused and realized that I did felt odd. The windows of the house were covered with something opaque. The house seemed to give off a heat, or a force, or maybe it was just my imagination. The hairs on the back of my neck stood as we approached the back door.

"Some of the grass back here is crushed. Someone has been here recently," Brady said.

"I'm going to kick the door in," I whispered to Brady. "I'll go in first. Wait for my word, okay?"

"Maybe we shouldn't do this. That's kind of breaking and entering, right?" Brady said.

"You can stay out here if you want."

"No. We're in this together."

I took a deep breath, turned around, and used the heel of my foot to kick the door open. I pushed Brady away before quickly stepping aside just in case someone was waiting with a gun.

I rushed in, scanning the small kitchen. Something approached at a high rate of speed. I ducked just as a skillet entered my path, flying over my head and clanging against the wall. I'd almost pulled the trigger out of fear and shock, but my brain quickly processed the shape on the other side of the room. A small woman was huddled in a corner. The light from a cellphone illuminated the empty, dim room.

"Krista Broussard?"

She looked up. Her eyes were red, and she was shaking.

"Please, don't kill me!" she wailed, a sob rushing through her body.

"We're not here to kill you. We just have a few questions. I'm a friend of Madalyn's," I said. Pulling out my wallet with one hand and showing her one of my business cards.

Krista stopped sobbing. "How do you know Madalyn?"

"I've worked with her in the past." I stepped closer to Krista. She flinched. I pulled out one of Madalyn's old business cards and handed it to Krista.

"Did she kill Nathan?"

"I was hoping you could answer that for me," I said, moving closer. This time, Krista didn't cower. I noticed a bag of chips, trail mix, and apples in a plastic sack on the floor. To downsize to this point, she had to be terrified.

"If Madalyn didn't do it, who did?" Krista asked.

I held out my hand. Krista hesitated, but eventually slipped her hand into mine. I gently helped her off the floor.

"We can keep you safe," I said.

"How do you know that? Who are you?" Krista asked, looking at Brady.

"This is Brady. He's helping me look into your husband's murder," I said, pointing at Brady. "I was a cop for several years up in Detroit. I'm a private investigator now. We could put you up somewhere safe." Brady and Krista shook hands. I looked around and wondered if Krista had been staying at the house since Nathan was murdered.

Brady and Krista shook hands. I looked around and wondered if Krista had been staying at the house since Nathan was murdered.

"I know. There's nothing here. I know. It's just the last place anyone would expect me to be."

"Why is that?" I asked.

"Nathan and I hadn't done anything with it for years. After Katrina came through, the place was in shambles. We were working on it, but it hadn't been a priority for a while."

"You guys have a lot of properties," I said.

"I don't keep up with all of that, but I think we have around twenty-five places."

"What happened to you and Nathan?" I asked, changing the subject.

"I was thinking about leaving, but I never would have killed him. He was a good man."

"We're going to need more details," I said calmly, hoping that my voice was reassuring.

"I wanted to wait until the New Year. My son's birthday is on December 29th and he's so close to Nathan. I just didn't want him to have to deal with his parents splitting so soon after his birthday. This isn't the first time I've thought about leaving, but

I was serious this time. I just couldn't do it yet. I gave her twenty thousand dollars so I wouldn't back out."

"The money was like a retainer?"

"No. I just knew if I gave her twenty thousand dollars to hold, I'd force myself to follow through."

"Why did you marry Nathan?" I asked.

"I married him because I thought I'd fallen in love with him," she said.

"Or did you marry him because he could provide a better life?"

"What do you mean?" Krista asked.

"I mean that beauty queens like a certain lifestyle and Nathan could afford to give you that."

"I was seventeen. I didn't know what I was doing. A night of drinks and fun turned into a baby and marriage. I thought I'd fall in love with him."

"Nathan was handsome and rich, and based on what I've read about him, he was also warm and caring."

"All that's true, but we weren't very compatible. We married young. I was in pageants and thought life would be different. I wanted to go to Hollywood and be a star, but one pageant in New Orleans changed everything."

"Why did you want to leave him?"

"I was tired of the political life. I just wanted to be normal. Nathan insisted on being a politician and it consumed his life. He wasn't around much, and I hated the way the media always wanted pictures. I was tired of it," Krista said.

"Was Nathan abusive?"

"Not in the way you're thinking."

"Krista, did Nathan put his hands on you?" I asked, taking a step forward and making eye contact. Krista shook her head.

"I just wanted out."

"So, you lied to Madalyn?"

"I didn't mean for any of this to happen."

"Well, it's pretty convenient that you wanted out and now your husband is dead."

"I didn't kill him. It must've been his brother."

"You think Grayson killed him?"

"Maybe. Their mother is on her last leg. She's not gonna make it much longer and his brother will inherit the fortune."

"Won't you get something?" I asked.

"Yes, but not as much as Grayson."

"You're the widow of his brother."

"Yes, but Grayson is the oldest boy, and he's his mother's favorite. He went into the ministry, which is what she wanted her boys to do, so now Grayson gets more. She changed the will after their father died. Nathan was a politician, which is the family business, but she hates it."

"How long have you been planning to leave him?"

"Not that long. Maybe since about May. I just wanted a different life. Look, I know I look bad right now, but it wasn't like that at all. I cared about Nathan. He was good to me, but my kids were thinking that lukewarm is how relationships should be. I don't want them to think that marriage isn't about love."

It was a valid concern. I hadn't expected that to be on her list of why she wanted to leave her husband. She seemed sincere, but why lie and say he was abusive?

"How do you know Madalyn Price?"

"That's a complicated story."

"Tell us anyway."

Krista sighed.

"I found out that she was coming to see Nathan every couple of months."

"Do you know why?"

Well, I found out why. Initially, I thought it was something bad, but Nathan often came across young women, mostly young moms, in abusive situations. He wanted to help them, and Madalyn has a reputation. I'm sure you know about her saving young girls."

"Yes. She's dedicated to helping young women get out of dangerous situations," I said.

"Nathan thought she could take a bunch of these women out of terrible relationships. Some of these women disappear off the grid. She seemed to be fantastic at what she did. I just thought it might be a way to get out."

"You have two children who are part of a dynasty. You're not being abused. Did you really think that you'd be able to just take off with Nathan's kids?"

Krista turned her back to us.

"You didn't plan on taking the kids," Brady said.

I looked at Brady. He folded his arms and said, "Let me guess. Madalyn kept mentioning the kids, and you didn't know how to break it to her that the kids weren't your concern."

"That's not true! I love my kids! Nathan would come to understand things in time, and we'd work out custody. You don't understand what it's like."

"We're not here to judge you. In fact, we really only need to know anything that has to do with Madalyn. Leaving the kids behind would have bothered Madalyn, so it's something we need to know," I said, giving Brady a quick look.

"I know little about her. Nathan raved about how she had a way of helping women who had previously refused help. That's all I needed to know."

"I don't always agree with her methods, but she definitely is good at what she does. Right now, she's sitting behind bars. This is a death penalty state and justice, from what I've heard, isn't always just in these parts," I said.

Krista nodded but remained silent.

"We need another suspect," Brady said. "Someone who might have hated your husband and wanted him dead. I bet it would help if you came out of the shadows and told the cops that Madalyn and Nathan were friends. All we need is a little reasonable doubt."

A few minutes passed before Krista said, "Okay. But I'm doing it my way."

"Of course," I said, though I wasn't sure what she meant.

"You never saw me. Leave here and don't tell anyone you saw me. Watch the news. I'll be on it."

14

———

We headed back to the car, climbed in, and sat in silence for a few minutes. I tried to formulate theories. Krista hiding out in a vacant house suggested she wasn't involved in Nathan's murder, but the fact that she gave Madalyn twenty thousand dollars was odd. Madalyn didn't charge women a fee when she helped them leave their abusive relationships.

"What are you thinking?" Brady asked.

"I think there's more to Krista Broussard, but we'll have to wait to find out."

"We're going to keep her secret?"

"Yes. I don't know if someone is after her, or what's going on, but I don't want to reveal her location, just in case."

"What if she's lying and hired someone to kill Nathan? She could have set Madalyn up."

"True, but I need more information before I conclude that."

"Alright. Well, what's next?"

"I've been looking at the area around Bayou Sauvage. There's a store right before you enter. I want to stop there and see if anyone remembers something from that night."

"Great. Let's go."

We climbed into the car and headed to Roscoe's Hut, the small store close to the bayou.

"I'll head inside. I'd like you to snoop around—pretend like we aren't together. See what you can see."

"Anything in particular you're looking for?" Brady asked.

I knew I was grasping at straws, but anything could help.

"Talk to anyone you run into, look to see if there's a back way from the store to the water, anything really. I'm at a loss."

Brady nodded, and we headed towards the Bayou Sauvage. There were a few buildings near Bayou Sauvage, but most were boarded up. A small store sat a couple of miles down the road from the pristine entrance to the preserve.

"Alright. Remember, we're looking for anything," I said, giving Brady a fist bump before getting out of the car.

The little store was more of a shack than a place you'd get food or other goods. They had tackle boxes, hooks and fishing poles, and other items one might need while out on the water. There was also a dusty shelf of overpriced trinkets and souvenirs in the back of the store. The owner was a man with flowing gray hair and a scruffy beard that reached the middle of his chest. He was changing the sign into front of the building to read, *Now serving food.* I watched his hands, layered in dirt, fiddling with the letters, and hoped that he wasn't the one cooking the grub.

"Hello," I said, causing the man to jump and turn around.

"You 'bout gave me my death. Hi. How can I help you?"

"I was wondering if you remember who came into your store between five and nine New Year's Eve."

"What, like surveillance? Naw, I ain't got none of that, but I was here that night. Let me guess. You wanna know who came in around the time of the Broussard murder?"

"Good guess. Yes, I'm looking into the murder of Nathan Broussard."

"Isn't everyone. You're the fourth person to show up asking questions."

I felt my eyebrows raise. "Really?"

"You want information and I want sales. What you buying?"

"What do you have?"

"Stuff. You like fruits and vegetables?"

"I do."

"I've got collards, lettuce, many greens."

"Kale?"

"Yeah. Two kinds of kale."

"I'll buy a few before I head out," I said.

"Now we're talking. Uriah. Nice to meet you, new customer," the man said, holding out his hand and letting out a laugh.

"Sylvia. Same here," I said, slipping my hand into his. "So, who came to ask questions?"

"A kid that worked for Broussard, the other Broussard, the pastor, and some cops. You want to know who asked the least important questions?"

"Who?"

"The cops," the man let out a loud cackle.

I forced out a giggle and a smile.

"Sorry about my mitts. They're a little are dirty," Uriah said, gently letting go of my hand. "Been out back in the garden. We're making food now and I'm growing as much as I can. I want it to be organic."

"Nice. What will you be serving?"

"Not too much. I'm going for a vegetarian vibe. People eat too much meat, so I'm just going to have your standard burger on the menu, but I really want to push the fruits and veggies."

Surprised, I nodded my head and asked a few more questions about his business endeavors before pulling out a picture of Madalyn.

"Did this woman come into the store that evening?"

"No, but apparently the cops wanted her to be in here. I tried to tell them that we sell mostly stuff for fishing and fixing things. We just started the food side because we're expanding to attract new people. Women included," Uriah said.

"Your clientele is mostly male?"

"Yep. The boys come in and get what they need and head out on their boats."

"Did Nathan Broussard come here often?"

"I don't think he ever been in here. He's a pretty boy type. Lots of money. He ain't going to be out there in a dinghy tryna catch dinner. But the pastor and the boy that come in asking questions, they both been in here before. And yes, before you ask, both the pastor and the boy were in New Year's Eve. I asked the pastor why he was asking questions if the police had already arrested the killer. He told me he's just trying to make sure that the police have the right person. That was odd. I guess he has reason to doubt that the cops have the right person."

"You know the pastor well?" I asked.

"Well enough. He's more a get your hands dirty type than his brother. He'd bring the young men from his church out here to fish. Nice enough, I guess. Friendly at least."

"What did the young man ask when he came in?"

"Basically, he was trying to rewrite history. He made some small talk and then he tried to get me to say he wasn't here on New Year's Eve."

"Why would he do that?"

"Because he was for sure in here that night," Uriah said.

"Was it busy?"

"No."

"You're sure he was here?"

"Yep. He had some trouble when he was younger, so people around here know him. I heard some scuttlebutt, but I don't know the facts, so I won't speak about it."

"What time did he come in?"

"5:30ish. I was thinking about closing up early when he came in."

"Do you remember what he bought?"

"I didn't until he came back in to ask questions. Now I recall he bought a box of gloves."

If Holden came in at 5:30, he had plenty of time to buy the gloves, shoot Nathan, and leave the area.

"Can you tell me what the pastor asked you?"

"Not too much. He just wanted to know who had been in here. He asked if I had surveillance cameras and I told him no. And before you ask, yes, I'm sure about all of this. I always work holidays, so my kids don't have to miss out on the festivities. They work here, too."

"Nice. A family business," I said.

"Yeah. They're going to keep it going after I'm gone."

"Great. So, you mentioned the cops were here. Would you mind sharing what they asked you?"

Uriah folded his arms over his chest.

"They had little to say. Mostly, they wanted me to tell them I'd seen that lady they arrested, but I hadn't. So, the conversation was short and sweet. I figured if they thought anything else was important, they would have asked. I guess you got a different thought about what's going on, huh?"

Now that I knew Holden had been in the store the night Nathan was killed, and Grayson had been in to question Uriah, I definitely had a different idea about the murder than the police.

"I like justice," I said.

"So do I. If that's what you're after, well, Godspeed. Things don't always go the right way around here. Be careful following up behind these guys. They don't always play fair."

15

———

I bought kale, onions, and potatoes from Uriah and headed back to the car. Brady was leaning against it.

"The kid isn't all that innocent," Brady said.

"Holden? I just heard the same thing."

"Yeah. People know him well around here. I talked with a lady who works at the preserve. She says a lot of trash accumulates around here, so the workers clean things up on this road. Apparently, Holden has been here asking questions."

"Yeah, the owner of the store told me the same thing," I said.

"Did he also fill you in on Holden's past?"

"He told me something happened, but he wasn't clear on the details."

"Holden got into some trouble when he was in high school. Looks like he got into a fight with a classmate and knocked the kid unconscious."

"Not good, but that's just typical teen behavior."

"The kid never woke up," Brady said.

"Oh no. That's terrible! There wasn't any type of sentence given?"

"Well, Holden had just turned eighteen. He was defending a girl from unwanted advances, and he was extremely remorseful. He comes from a decent family and they're super religious, so the judge gave him a break. It also didn't hurt that a beloved politician went to bat for the kid."

"Nathan put his two cents into the case?"

"Yeah, and it worked. The story didn't get much press. The lady told me I'd probably have to really dig to find much about it."

"I wonder how Nathan's involvement went over with the parents of the kid that died?"

"Probably not well."

"Wow. We'll have to see what's out there. The store owner told me that Holden came here on New Year's Eve and purchased gloves. He also came back after the murder and tried to convince Uriah, the owner, that he wasn't here that night."

"Interesting."

"Also, the police came by and tried to get Uriah to say that he'd seen Madalyn, but he says she wasn't here that night. He works holidays so his kids can have those days off, so he would know if she came in."

"So, Holden Timmons is shaping up to be a bit of a suspect. Seemed pretty eager to speak with us."

"He did. He was also nervous about us speaking to Darcy, the girl that worked on Nathan's campaign with him."

"We need to find her."

"I called her the other day. No answer. She'll get another call as soon as we're done here."

"Good. Oh, I also found out that the guy that found the body is named Bruce. He's a volunteer, and he's in the office today."

"Excellent! Thanks, Brady. Let's go see what Bruce has to say."

Bᴀʏᴏᴜ Sᴀᴜᴠᴀɢᴇ ᴡᴀs a beautiful and haunting location inside the city. With bottomland hardwoods and brackish marshes, it was the perfect place to meet for conversations, or for a stroll through nature. Just natural enough to feel you're outside of the city, but close enough to an urban center to dip in and spend a few hours before heading back to the big city.

A small office sat to the left of the entrance of the visitors' center. We parked in front of the building and headed inside. A man dressed in camouflage was bent over an old, wooden desk. He looked up as the screen door creaked closed.

"May I help you?" the man asked.

"Yes, we're looking for a man named Bruce."

"Why?"

"We'd like to ask him a few questions," I said.

"Who are you?" the man asked. His eyes were full of suspicion.

"My name is Sylvia Wilcox, and this is Brady Kepler. We'd like to ask a few questions about the incident that took place on New Year's Eve."

"You mean the murder? Are you here on behalf of the victim or the perpetrator?"

"We're here on behalf of justice and truth."

"Hmm. Okay. I'll bite. What do you want to know?"

"Can you share what you saw that night?"

"Sure. The cops know all of this and it's all over the news."

"I was a police officer in Detroit at one time. I know how useful it can be to talk through scenarios."

Bruce abandoned whatever he was ruffling through on the desk and turned to face me.

"You were a cop?"

"Yes."

His shoulders relaxed, and he let out a sigh of relief. "I

thought you were a reporter pretending to be some type of investigator."

"I am a private investigator now, but I was a cop for five years," I said, pulling a business card from my wallet.

Bruce examined the card, his brow wrinkled.

"I recently retired. Bruce Carpenter," Bruce said, his demeanor softening. "Glad to meet you two. Now, how can I help?"

"First, it would be good to know more about Bayou Sauvage."

"Well, as you can see, it's in an interesting area. The surrounding neighborhood, New Orleans East, isn't some place that's shy about violence. People die in this part of town frequently. It's not an awful place to dump a body, but the gators aren't out at this time of year. It's also a nature reserve, so someone is always patrolling the area."

"You were on patrol the night Nathan Broussard's body was found?"

Bruce folded his arms. "Yes. I was having a great time. Looking forward to spending the night hanging out with my family and friends. Something just told me to do one more pass. I grew up in the bayou. Now I live in the city, so I like to get my feel when I'm here volunteering."

"Do many crimes take place here?"

"Petty drug dealing, homeless people sleeping close by, and sometimes kids will come down here and cause trouble, but mostly, things stay calm on this end."

"The place where the body was is not considered federal waters, correct?"

"Yeah. It was outside of the area where I usually patrol."

"Any reason you went further that night?"

Bruce's brow creased. "I can go further. I just usually don't."

Not exactly an answer.

"How often do you venture outside of your boundaries?"

"I don't have boundaries. I can go where I want," Bruce said, sounding irritated.

"Of course. I just was wondering if something piqued your interest that day. Did you see something out of the ordinary?"

Bruce's brow relaxed. He sighed and took a deep breath.

"Listen, I was just trying to get a little extra time on the water. I've been retired for a little while now, but it's still hard. I miss the job. So, when I come here, I try to make the most of it. That night, I was just feeling nostalgic. I'm happy to be retired, but New Year's Eve was a night I always worked. I miss my past, but I like my present, too. The pull between the past and the present was enjoyable. So, I went a little longer than I should have. It wasn't planned."

"Okay. Would you mind walking me through what you saw that night?"

"I was just about to turn around when I saw a woman in the water."

"What was the woman doing?"

"She was in the water. It looked like she was trying to get someone on to shore, but it's tricky in that area. The land isn't stable."

"What made you think the woman was pulling someone out?" I asked.

"The woman was small. She was pulling on something, but she was struggling. I guess I was curious about what she was doing."

"You were a cop for thirty years. Why would a killer be dragging a body out of the water?"

Bruce waited a minute before saying, "They wouldn't."

"Right. It's very hard to get evidence from a body after it's been in the water for a while. It's also common for bodies in the water to get lost and turn up years later, which makes them hard to identify."

"Pulling the body out of the water isn't in the killer's best interest. Not only do they risk being seen, they also are increasing the chances of identification."

"And Madalyn is small. Why would she try to pull a dead body out of the water?"

Bruce nodded. "It's a good question."

"Maybe she was trying to save him," Brady added.

Bruce and I looked at Brady.

"Did you see anything else? Was there anyone else in the area?" I asked.

"There was one thing. I didn't pay much attention then, but now that I'm thinking about it, I wish I had."

I waited for Bruce to gather his thoughts. His forehead was creased. It looked like he was trying to figure out exactly what he wanted to say.

"There was a little dinghy on the water that night. I saw it out of the corner of my eye. The boat was too small to be out as far as they were. I was dreaming of going home. I grew up near Port Allen. It was pretty small when I lived there. Used to spend my days on the river with my dad and brother. I probably should have paid more attention or checked on them, but I was drifting back into my boyhood."

"This is a nice retirement job. Nothing wrong with enjoying it," I said, reassuring Bruce.

"The boat was small. Had a catchy name, but I can't remember what it was." Bruce closed his eyes.

After a few minutes, I said, "You can call me later if the name comes to you."

"Yeah. Okay. So, what's your connection to the suspect?"

"I've worked with her in the past."

"Hell of a lot to go through for a coworker."

"Well, truth is truth. Justice is important."

"I agree. Can I run a theory by you?"

"Please."

"The woman was trying to pull the body out of the water.

And like you said, no killer wants a body back on land. Even that night, I got the feeling Nathan Broussard meant something to this woman."

"You question whether this woman is the killer?"

"I have questions. I don't know if she's the killer, but I know water is a killer's friend."

"Agreed. Do you remember anything else about that day?"

Bruce Carpenter closed his eyes for a moment.

"There were two other boats out in the area. I can't remember much right now, but I'll call you if I recall anything else."

16

———————

The next morning, I called Darcy a second time. This time, she answered on the third ring.

"I'm sorry that I didn't get back to you, but I've been busy," Darcy said. Her voice was thin, and her speech sounded rushed.

"No worries. I would like to speak with you about the night Nathan Broussard was murdered. Are you available today?"

"Well, I have church in a little, but maybe after that."

"Okay. What time works?"

Darcy was quiet for a few moments. I heard a car door close in the background and a car engine start.

"I don't know how I could help. I'm sorry about Mr. Nathan's death," a soft, shy voice filled the phone.

"Sometimes, people know things that are helpful, and they don't even realize it. I promise I won't take much of your time. Will noon work?"

I waited for a response. After what felt like several minutes, Darcy said, "One-ish. I have a church and brunch after that. I work at three so I won't have much time, but I can meet you near the Pastry Peddler—that's where I work. There's a pier nearby."

BRADY STAYED at the hotel and searched for information on a connection between Holden and Nathan. I headed to a small park on the Mississippi. The same woman I'd seen at the church with Holden and his family was standing at the edge of the water. Darcy was short and full figured, with an apple shaped face. She looked up as I approached. I smiled and nodded to put her at ease.

"Darcy?"

"That's me," she said, folding her arms and tapping one foot.

"I'm Sylvia Wilcox. Thank you for meeting with me."

"No problem. Although, I don't know anything about Mr. Broussard's murder."

"Okay. Well, let's just talk about what you were doing that day."

"What? Am I a suspect?" Darcy asked, her green eyes filled with fear.

"Remember Darcy, I'm not a cop."

Her shoulders rose and fell, and she let out a heavy sigh.

"Right. I'm sorry. This is all so weird. Mr. Broussard was a good man."

"That is one reason why I want to make sure the right person pays for murdering him," I said, moving toward a picnic table. Darcy followed and sat opposite me.

"I heard the killer is already in jail," Darcy said in a hushed tone.

"Innocent until proven guilty is my philosophy."

Darcy tilted her head. "You're right. I'm jumping the gun. Anyway, what would you like to know?"

"What did you do the day Nathan Broussard was murdered?"

"Nothing special. I got up and went to the campaign office because we had some paperwork to do and a meeting. Holden and I were going to appear at a parade the next day and canvas for Mr. Broussard. We went over some ideas to get people over to our booth. I think we finished up around noon."

"Did you leave the office after that?"

Darcy titled her head and waited before answering. "It's hard to remember. That day seems so far away now, but I think we hung around for a while and came up with some strategies to get people interested in talking politics with us."

"What type of strategies did you come up with?"

"Just your run-of-the-mill stuff. Nothing major. Start off talking about the Super Bowl and segue into politics. I needed some pointers on the sports angle."

"Where were you the night Nathan Broussard was murdered?"

"I was at a party that night. Some of his friends threw a little get together. Nothing major."

"That's great. What time did the party start?"

"Early. There were games on that the boys were watching and some of us girls were just hanging out and chatting."

"When you say early..."

"I guess I showed up around five."

"What time did you leave the campaign office?"

"Maybe around three?"

Nathan was at the bayou at 5:30. Darcy wasn't really a suspect, but no one had been ruled out in my book.

"Do you remember what you did between the time you left the office and went to the party?"

"Went home and got ready."

"Where was the party?"

"It was in Slidell on the lake. Some guy Holden knew was throwing the party, but I don't remember his name."

"What time did Nathan arrive?"

"Um, I don't remember. I was already there having a good time."

"How long did you stay at the party?" I asked.

"Um... I wasn't keeping track. I was drinking so I kind of got lost in the night. You know what I mean?"

"How much did you drink that evening?"

Darcy lowered her head.

"I'm not here to judge. I just want to know if you were able to remember what happened that night," I said.

"Um, no. I couldn't remember much. There was a game of beer-pong early on. Then, Bacardi shots and some Hurricanes. Eventually, I ended up passed out in the basement."

"Any idea what time that was?"

"Not really. It really is all a blur," Darcy said, her cheeks turning red.

"What time did you leave?"

"Um..."

"This is important, Darcy."

She bit her lip.

"Whatever you tell me stays between us," I said, doing my best to keep my voice calm and reassuring.

"Holden took care of me, so I... stayed there that night. Nothing happened. He just took me to a room and put me to bed. When I woke up the next day, the door was locked, and I was fine."

"Did you see Holden that morning?"

"No. He left me a nice note, but he wasn't there when I woke up," Darcy ran a hand over her forehead before saying, "Ma'am?"

"Yes?"

"Please don't tell Pastor Grayson about this. He helped me

get my job at the Pastry Peddler and he hooked me up with the volunteer opportunity for Mr. Broussard's campaign. He's been so good to me. I don't want to hurt him."

Darcy's eyes were wide with fear.

"No worries. There is no need for him to know. Is there anything else you can tell me about the party?"

"No, but I can state that Holden would never hurt anyone."

"That's good to know," I said, realizing that Darcy and Holden were both eager to protect one another.

"Have you met Krista Broussard?"

"Yeah, but I don't know her well. She would come by the office every now and then and bring us cookies or cakes. Sweet lady, from what I could see. Quiet, though. I heard she is missing. Is that true?"

"The local news says she hasn't turned up."

"But they arrested the killer... I mean suspect. Why would Mrs. Broussard be missing?"

I let Darcy mull over the question.

"There were rumors. I never believed them, but some people swore by them," Darcy said as she picked at invisible lint on her dress.

"What type of rumors?"

"Some people thought that Pastor Grayson and Mr. Nathan had gotten into it about their daddy's money. Ethel thought it was because of their wives."

"Was there a rift between the brothers' wives?"

"It depends on what you mean by rift. They didn't associate with each other at church, and you'd only know they were in the same family when the brothers were together. They were very different and almost acted like strangers."

"How long have you been going to Rise and Aspire?"

"Just a few months. Holden really likes it there," Darcy said, doing her best to smile.

"How do you feel about it?"

"My parents are very religious, but I'm not so sure about things. Once I get married and have children, I'll be more into it, but right now, I want to live my life."

I nodded. "Sounds reasonable."

"The sermons aren't good. Pastor Grayson is so nice, but I have to have a few coffees to keep me up unless he screams. If not for that, I'd be knocked out."

I considered asking why she continued to attend, but I knew the answer.

"Well, there must be some that like Pastor Grayson's sermons. He recently moved to a bigger campus," I said.

"That was something I thought Mr. Nathan and Pastor Grayson might have fought about."

"Why is that?"

"Mr. Nathan was very diplomatic, but you could tell he didn't like Rise and Aspire. He smiled and was supportive, but he never looked happy. And I heard him grumble a time or two about the cost of the place. He thought the place was way too big."

"Interesting. Thank you for that information. What else can you tell me—"

"Ms. Wilcox."

A man's voice filled my ears. I turned around and froze.

"Mr. Broussard," I said, doing my best to hide the shock I felt.

"Pastor Grayson, at your service," he said, giving a salute before reaching out for my hand. "I hear that you're looking into my brother's murder."

"That's right," I said.

"Darcy, you're done here," Grayson said, casting a look of disappointment behind me.

"Darcy, you don't have to leave," I countered, staring at Grayson.

"Ms. Wilcox, Darcy is part of my flock. I am the shepherd, and I will tend to my sheep. Darcy, depart."

I heard the young woman scurry away.

"Now that's more like it," Grayson said. "I haven't had a conversation with you, Ms. Wilcox. Neither has my wife. I've heard that you attended church on Sunday. Why didn't you talk to me then?" Grayson moved closer. I stepped back.

"Pastors are busy on Sundays. Not only do they have multiple services, but they also mingle with the congregation and take care of concerns people have. I didn't want to interrupt your spiritual flow."

Grayson laughed. "Do you know the Lord, Ms. Wilcox?"

"I do."

"You sure?"

"Let's just say I'm comfortable with what I know," I said, feeling a bit put off with the line of questioning.

"Alright. I'd like for you to come back to church on Sunday and fellowship with us. No need to hide in the shadows like you did last week."

"Thank you for the invitation. I will keep it in mind," I said, taking another step back. Had Darcy told Grayson we were meeting? If so, had she intended for him to come and rescue her from the interview? Or had he somehow found out Darcy and I were meeting on his own?

"Well, you could talk with Audrey at the church. You just met with Darcy. It seems like you're curious about all of us."

It was uncomfortable to know that Grayson was aware of my meeting with Darcy, and that I'd been at his church, even though I'd used a false name and tried my best to stay in the shadows.

"Mr. Broussard, I'd be happy to meet with you and your wife," I said.

"I'm glad to hear that. I will expect you at the church in the next twenty minutes. I would talk to you here, but Audrey is eager to have her say, as well," Grayson said, walking away before I accepted or reject the invitation.

He was arrogant and annoying, but it was very rare that a person of interest volunteered to speak with a private investigator. I had to take Grayson up on the offer. I looked around for Darcy, but she was nowhere to be seen. Before driving off, I called Brady.

"Sylvia, you need to get back here as soon as possible. Krista Broussard is on the news. You will not believe what she's saying."

"I'll be there in a little while, but guess who showed up while I was meeting with Darcy?"

"Who?"

"Grayson. I'm headed to the church to talk with him. Then I'll be there."

"Hurry. See you soon."

17

———

I parked in front of Rise and Aspire Church. The large lot was empty except for two cars, which I assumed were Grayson and Audrey's vehicles. I was glad I'd called Brady and let him know where I was going. Grayson probably would not kill me, but I was already creeped out that the pastor had turned up out of the shadows. As I stepped out of the car, the front door of the church opened.

"Ms. Wilcox, I am so thankful that you are taking an interest in my brother's death," Grayson said, meeting me at the edge of the sidewalk, reaching out his hand. We'd already shared a shake at the park. I hesitated.

"I'm sorry to interrupt you and Darcy. She's a young woman in need of direction. It was rude to just show up, but let's call a truce. I'm just here to help," Grayson pushed his hand closer. I reluctantly gave him a shake. He might reveal valuable information. I needed to play nice.

"What would you like to share with me?"

"I would have done it earlier if you'd only called me up or stopped by to chat after service the other day. Nathan and I were very close. He was my little brother."

I nodded. Grayson still had my hand in a tight grip. It was uncomfortable, but he wasn't taking the gentle pulls as a sign the handshake needed to end.

"Come on into my sanctuary. Let's get some god-light on the situation. He can illuminate anything. Amen."

Grayson turned and took off toward the church, still holding my hand. I walked slowly, purposely trying to end the hand holding. It was strange, but I kept my cool.

"We better pray first," he said, bowing his head and reaching for my other hand. I reluctantly gave it to him and bowed my head, keeping my eyes open.

"Thank you, Lord, for being here with us today. Please send your blessing upon this conversation Lord. Thank you for bringing us together for this talk. I want to thank you, Lord, for all you've done and all you're going to do for us right now. Thank you, Lord. Thank you, Lord!"

I kept my head bowed out of respect, but I'd never heard a prayer like that. Darcy was right. Grayson might be in the wrong field.

After a few more amens, Grayson said, "I have a lot of pain over my little brother's death. I am very suspicious of my sister-in-law."

Before I could respond, a petite woman with a quick splash of red hair, freckles on her cheeks, and large, green eyes entered the room. She wore a tan fitted suit, with the skirt reaching just below her knee, and sensible matching pumps. Audrey shook her head as she headed in our direction.

"You don't have to look very far. You know who did this," the woman said, wagging her finger.

"Honey, now we don't want to accuse Krista of anything yet. We need facts," Grayson said.

"Who else would do this? Why is she missing? Come on Grayson, let's be honest."

Grayson finally let go of my hand and slipped his arm around his wife's shoulders.

"Ms. Wilcox, this is my beautiful and feisty wife, Audrey. As you can see, she has strong opinions. I, for one, think we need to be very suspicious of my sister-in-law, but I want more information before we accuse her of anything. With that said, it seems like she almost had a plan."

"Almost?" Audrey said, sticking a hand on her hip.

"Sweetheart... We have to remain objective."

"But we know who murdered Nathan. Why pretend?"

"Mrs. Broussard, I don't know who murdered Nathan. That's why I'm here talking to you," I said.

Audrey turned to me.

"Where are my manners?" she pushed a wayward strand of hair off her forehead and said, "I'm Audrey. Pleased to meet you, Ms. Wilcox."

We shook hands.

"Nice to meet you, as well. Now, I'd love to hear why you're so sure Krista was involved in Nathan's death."

Audrey folded her hands and began telling the story.

"Krista was dying to get out of that marriage. She was so ready to leave Nathan. It was sad to watch how disenchanted she was with the family. Especially since Nathan was a good, hard-working family man. She wanted her freedom either to be with someone else, or to be free of responsibility. There were no other reasons. Nathan was never mean to her, and he was an all-around great guy."

"So, you believe Krista is responsible, even though someone else was found with Nathan's body?"

"Sit down, ma'am, because I've got a lot to get out."

I took a seat.

"I'm telling you Krista didn't enjoy being a mother or a wife. She wanted to go back to that little town in Tennessee where she was born and live in a trailer with the rest of her family. She hated having to be a decent human because of Nathan's career. Krista wanted to be in the trailer park drinking, smoking cigarettes, and not having to worry about even getting up in the morning and letting people photograph her."

The sisters-in-law were not friends, but Krista had been a beauty pageant contestant. Was Audrey's opinion based on Krista not being from a wealthy background? I let Audrey take the lead and talk as much as she wanted.

"Let me tell you how this all went down. Nathan was a young man, living his life and building his career. Me and Grayson had only been married a little while, but we were high school sweethearts, so I watched Nathan grow up. He was fresh out of college, young and trying to build a platform. Twenty-two, living life well, and trying to follow in his father's footsteps, as a politician and CEO of the family business. A beauty pageant came to town and Nathan was asked to be one of the judges. He was iffy about it because he was paving the way for a political career, and he didn't want to seem trivial, you know what I mean?"

I nodded and waited for more from Audrey.

"A young man judging a beauty contest might seem shallow or sexist, but Nathan was nothing like that. It would give him more exposure, so he did it. Well, there was a beautiful woman there. She stole his heart and like many young men, he spent an evening with her and after having a good time, if you know what I mean, she mentions that she's sixteen. Immediately, Nathan was scandalized. He got right out of that hotel room and rushed home. Eventually, he told Grayson the story, who, of course, told me, and I said, 'Oh no. Expect a phone call.' Sure enough, a few months later, the call came. Krista, the sixteen-year-old, was pregnant."

"So, this was a shotgun wedding?"

"She was going to be seventeen in a few months, which is the legal age of consent in Louisiana. So, Nathan did the only thing he could do. He paid for her care, made sure she was getting good prenatal, and after the baby was born, they got married. Of course, a reporter found out and got the news out there. A few weeks after the wedding, the same reporter caught them in the backyard with little Nathan Jr. That's how it all started. Once Nathan was in the office, there were plenty of questions about Krista's age and how they met. It was a big ole mess for him and it led to a bunch of petty stories about our family."

"Thank you for sharing that information, Mrs. Broussard. What else can you two tell me about Nathan and Krista's relationship?"

"They were together and happy enough for a time, but Krista is a free spirit. She doesn't like the cameras, lights, action part of politics. She was a kid when they got together, but that was twelve years ago. She's changed over time," Grayson said.

"Krista is twenty-eight now?"

"Yeah. My poor brother had his birthday a few weeks ago. Just turned thirty-five. He had so much life left in him." Grayson said.

"I'm so sorry Nathan is gone."

"So are we. We're glad someone is looking into this," Audrey said.

"We feel like the police don't want to listen to what we have to say. They arrested somebody, and they wanted to put it on this poor woman, but I just don't believe it. This might've been somebody who was helping Nathan with something, but I know Nathan would never step out on his wife, and I also know that Krista is the one that wanted him gone."

"So, you and Grayson had the children that night, right?"

"We still have them. Krista dropped them off on New Year's Eve at noon. Nothing happens on New Year's Eve until the evening, but she decided, 'Let's get these kids out here as soon as possible' and, of course, I was at home, so I told her she could bring them over. She rushed out, claiming she had to go shopping or something, which I knew was a lie."

"Why didn't you think she was being honest?"

"Because Nathan had a maid for her, and Krista never does the shopping. She's not a domesticated woman. She doesn't even cook. I knew she was lying, but I don't enjoy her company, so I let her go."

"Did she mention what she and Nathan did that evening?"

Audrey shook her head. "No. I regret it now, but I didn't ask. I just wanted her out."

"Audrey and Krista have never gotten along well," Grayson added.

"You want to know what the kids have been doing? Crying day and night for their daddy. Do you want to know how many times they've asked about their mom? Twice," Audrey said, not waiting for me to respond to her question.

"Calm down, sweetie," Grayson said, running a hand over his wife's back. Audrey turned her face up towards her husband and kissed him on the cheek.

"I'm okay, honey. I just want her to understand how Krista was."

"Any ideas where Krista might be?" I asked.

Audrey turned back to face me. "I think she went back to Tennessee. She was probably just waiting for the insurance check to arrive. But first, she'll have to be in the clear. Honestly, I don't think that's going to happen."

"Mr. Broussard, what can you tell me about your parents?"

"Daddy has been with the Lord for a long time now. Momma is very sick and now that Nathan is gone, I don't see her carrying on much longer. Her and Nathan didn't really see eye to eye. I'm closer to her, but Momma always regretted the distance between her and Nathan. She wanted to make things better before she died. To be honest, Nathan wasn't interested in doing that. My little brother held a grudge."

"Was Nathan close to your father?"

"Boy, was he. Nathan was so close to Daddy. I think he came along after Momma was done with babies. Daddy was excited and Nathan became his little buddy. They were like two peas in a pod. You can tell it by the career paths that we chose. Nathan followed Daddy into politics, and I've always been a churchgoer like Momma. No family is without problems, of course."

"Did Nathan do anything else before he went into politics?"

"He went to law school, but he never really practiced law. He went right into office after that."

"How old was Nathan when he took office?"

"Twenty-six. He graduated from law school, worked the business with Daddy, and ran fresh out of law school. He was very popular and was definitely going to win the upcoming election," Grayson said.

"A C.E.O. who is also a politician can generate a lot of enemies. Were there people who might have wanted to hurt Nathan?"

"Not that I know of. Maybe that strange fella that was running against him."

"You are now running against Mr. Gilles, correct?"

Grayson titled his head. He seemed taken aback by the question.

"Remember, I was here when you made the announcement on Sunday."

"That's right. I almost forgot about your stealthy visit. Nathan wanted to keep things the same way they have always been, and I want the same. That's why I'm running."

"What about the family businesses? Are you running those as well?"

Again, Grayson gave me a look that told me I knew more than he thought I did.

"Ms. Wilcox, you certainly have done your homework. Nathan and I ran the company together."

"50/50?"

"What does this have to do with Nathan's murder?" Audrey asked.

"It helps to have a clear picture of someone's life and finances."

I wondered how things were divvied up in the will. The Broussards had several companies. I knew about the real estate arm, the oil company, the politics, and the church, but something told me there was more to this.

"Honey, you have that appointment, right? I can finish up with Ms. Wilcox," Audrey said, looked towards the back of the church.

Darla and Chuck Timmons were walking down the aisle.

"Hey, Ms. Wilcox," Darla Timmons called to me, waving her hands in the air.

"Hello Mr. And Mrs. Timmons," I said, giving them a smile."

"You three know each other, huh?" Grayson said. "Well, I've got to get going here. Ms. Wilcox, I hate to take off, but running a church takes a lot. We've got to get ready for Bible study. It's been a pleasure."

Grayson and I shook hands before he walked briskly across the auditorium and out the side door. He'd invited me to the church to talk with him. Now, he said he had a previously scheduled appointment. Clearly, he didn't want to discuss the money situation.

"He has so much to do," Audrey said, smiling, but her eyes looked nervous. The question about the family business had changed the dynamic.

"Just a few more questions and I'll let you go, Mrs. Broussard."

"Alright," she said, glancing at an enormous clock that sat on the wall behind her. "I need to be somewhere in about fifteen minutes."

Now she also had an upcoming appointment. I racked my brain for good questions. This would probably be the last time the Broussards agreed to speak with me.

I nodded and asked. "Where do you and Grayson live?"

Another unexpected question. Krista narrowed her eyebrows.

"We live in Slidell. We got the water, and it's far enough from the cities that we don't see the crime. And obviously, the church is right outside of Slidell, so that works well."

Across the water. Not too far from where Nathan's body was found.

18

Brady was standing in front of the laptop when I got back. His eyes were wide.

"Watch this," Brady said, turning the laptop to face me and pressing play on a video. A reporter with a concerned look on her face walked toward the camera.

"Krista Broussard appeared at the police department this morning with a wild tale. We don't have all the details, but she claims that she was kidnapped and recently got free. Now, what we don't know is if the suspect the police arrested and released on bail is involved in this kidnapping plot. Mrs. Broussard was sobbing and disheveled when she showed up at the precinct and, according to sources, she was terrified. The former teenage beauty queen is still inside answering questions, and we are waiting for an official announcement from the chief."

"Kidnapped? Are you kidding me? What is she doing? No one is going to believe she was kidnapped while her kids just spent the night with their cousins and her husband was murdered. She told me I'd see her on the news, but I definitely didn't expect this," I said.

"Right. Also, I've been doing some checking and Grayson

Broussard is not good with money. There are several articles about the church and how it's not doing well. He also has a bunch of inactive LLCs he's set up over the years. There seems to have been a bit of a rift in the family because Grayson was bringing unconventional aspects into his services."

"Like what?"

"Snake handlers and faith healers at the church, and some type of weird insurance presentation from a guy who eventually went to jail for fraud."

"That lines up with what happened when I brought up the family business with him and his wife. Grayson didn't like that. He actually left the interview and when I continued along that line of questioning with his wife, she suddenly had somewhere else she had to be."

"Really? Well, there's some speculation that Grayson used public funds to build the church. This was never proven, but it caused some issues for Nathan a few years ago."

"That's a motive," I said.

"Also, their mother was a major supporter of the church before she got sick. There are a lot of pictures of her and Grayson in the newspapers. Not that many of her with Nathan."

"That aligns with what Grayson said. The mom is closer to Grayson, which gives Krista a motive. And that she's lying about being kidnapped is an ominous sign."

"So, you think this is a family affair?"

"Not sure, but here's another interesting tidbit. Grayson and Audrey live in Slidell. Audrey mentioned the water. What are the odds they have a boat?"

"There are no odds. They have a boat. I'm sure of it. Probably more than one."

"Let's think about this. Grayson starts a church, and it's not going well. His mother is very sick, and she's possibly going to die soon. If Nathan is dead, the company will most likely go to

Grayson. He says that he and Nathan ran the company together, but I'm willing to bet it's not a 50/50 split."

"One responsible brother and the other struggling to find his way."

"That's exactly what it sounds like."

"I also did some research on the oil industry here."

"What did you find?" I asked.

"The project Lucian's company wants to start will take place in an area just out of where Nathan was found. I doubt Madalyn is involved with this, but Nathan could have gone there to meet someone, maybe even Lucian, and something happened."

"Or Lucian sent someone to take care of Nathan."

"What's the Krista angle?"

"I don't know what to think. After we talked with her, I thought she was being honest. Now that she's gone to the police claiming to have been abducted, I'm not sure what to think."

"So, there's one more thing," Brady said.

"What else?"

"Nathan was thirty-five, and he's from a prominent family. Does that remind you of something?"

I thought for a moment.

"Humor me. What should I be thinking of?"

"The ghost tour. Remember? The curse."

"Brady, we're really busy right now. We don't have time for fun."

"It's not fun I'm thinking of. What if the Broussards are the family that got cursed?"

I shook my head. "I can't believe you're still thinking that was true."

"Well, listen to this. Nathan and Grayson had an uncle that died at twenty-two. There was also a great uncle who disappeared on a safari when he was thirty. He was never seen again and presumed dead."

"Okay. I'll play along. Did any other family members die young?"

"Yeah. The great uncle was one of three siblings that died."

"Right. Life was more dangerous back then. People died of diseases, freak accidents, and wounds."

"True, but you want to know what happened to their uncle?"

"Not really but tell me any way."

"He was partying in the French Quarter one night and didn't make it home. No one really knows what happened, his death was horrific, and the police speculated that he was enticed into some type of séance and the group he was with decided to take him out. I'll save you the gory details, but they only recovered a few limbs."

"Goodness. I shouldn't have left you here by yourself. So, you're saying that we're dealing with voodoo?"

Brady folded his arms and creased his brow.

"I'm not saying that, but it is curious, right? The Broussard family members that died all met their end by thirty-five. It's just strange that we heard a story about a family being cursed and the youngest sons were destined to die by thirty-five."

I couldn't deny that it was shocking to hear that three generations of the Broussards had lost young men. But it could all be coincidence.

"Let's call Martin. Maybe he has something for us."

"I WAS JUST ABOUT to call you. You will not believe this," Martin said.

"Okay. Lay it on me," I said, switching the phone to speaker so Brady could hear.

"I talked to Kara. Carson and Madalyn were trying to have a relationship of the romantic variety. It got messy, and they broke it off. Well, kind of. Carson wanted Madalyn to stop doing something. Kara doesn't know what that something was."

"I bet Carson wanted her to stop the rescues," I said.

"Yeah, that's what I'm thinking. Also, Madalyn didn't get fired from her professorship. She told them she was taking a hiatus. So, the charges Carson filed didn't affect her employment because, technically, she wasn't employed at the university, so she didn't have to report it."

"She gave up everything to rescue women and children full time."

"Well, she was still doing yoga, but that is one of her connections to find women that need to be rescued from bad situations, so I guess that was the only thing that could stay."

"What about Danica?"

"Danica and Kara live together. It seems that the half-sisters have developed a strong bond. They're both attending State and doing well, but they came to town after they heard Madalyn was in jail. The kids are close, so I guess it makes sense that Carson and Madalyn got together. What doesn't make much sense is that they didn't work out," Martin said.

"Yeah. Kind of seems like a no-brainer."

"According to both girls, things are going well. They thought they were all going to be one big family."

"That sounds so odd. I guess there was a time when I suspected that they might be together, but that was years ago."

"Kara told me there was talk of a wedding."

"A wedding? Oh my gosh, I feel so out of the loop. Okay, let's piece this together. We've got Madalyn rescuing women and children, but also visiting New Orleans every few months around holidays. Carson doesn't like that Madalyn is involved in risky business, but he wants a future with her. But eventually he files some domestic disturbances. What is the point of that?"

"No idea. Doesn't make any sense," Martin said.

"Well, it could make sense," Brady piped in.

"Really? How so?" I asked.

"Yeah, I can't see a way it makes total sense," Martin said. "Give us your angle, Brady."

"What if Carson is trying to get Madalyn into a position where she needs to depend on him?"

"Why would he want that?" I asked.

"It's very simple. Here's the thing. You've got a beautiful, determined, and successful woman that you'd like to settle down with, but you know she's seriously independent, and probably a little scared of commitment. If you can get her to stop doing the thing that she uses as an excuse for not being in a relationship with you, maybe she'll settle down with you. After a while, a guy gets desperate."

"Sounds familiar," Martin said. "I think this is a conversation the two of you should have alone. Should I hang up?"

"No," I said. "Brady, thank you for that analysis. It fits Madalyn very well. Moving on," I said, clearing my throat. "So, here's the deal. We've got Carson trying to sabotage Madalyn's rescue empire because he wants to settle down with her, a dead husband, who is also a prominent politician, and Madalyn had twenty thousand dollars cash on her when they found her. But I don't think any of that has to do with Nathan's murder. Grayson is very controlling. He either followed Darcy to our meeting, or he has her trained to tell him if an outsider contacts her."

"What happened at your meeting?" Brady asked.

"Well, I was talking with Darcy, who says that she doesn't remember anything from New Year's Eve. She was explaining how terrible Grayson is as a pastor and suddenly, Grayson was standing behind me."

"That's creepy," Martin said. "What did he want?"

"Actually, he wanted me to leave Darcy and go to his church to talk with him and his wife."

"Did you go?" Brady asked.

"Yes. He told Darcy to leave, and since I figured he wants to talk with me, I took him up on the offer. How many people want to talk with a P.I.?"

"Good point. What did you find out?" Martin asked.

"Grayson and his wife didn't enjoy talking about money or his profession, and both told me they are suspicious of Krista. Based on what she told the police, she definitely didn't tell us everything."

"Sounds like she's putting on a show. She can't have people thinking she didn't care about the kids. That would make people wonder if she felt the same way about Nathan."

"Yeah, she took great offense when you suggested she was abandoning her children," I said.

"Was she leaving the kids behind?" Martin asked.

"Yep. Brady called her out and she got angry," I said, suddenly realizing how tired I was. "I don't have anything right now. Let's sleep on it, and we'll regroup tomorrow."

19

____

Shadows. The hint of something moving about. Quiet, but the weight of the shape could be felt. Something or someone was close.

I woke up startled, sitting up in the darkness. Had I dreamt that someone else was in the room? Or was there another person in the room? I reached over in the bureau drawer and pulled out my revolver. Holding the gun out in front of me, I scanned the room. My eyes adjusted to the dark. Something moved. I held my breath, listening for abnormalities in the silence. A quiet creak whispered in the night. I stood up in the bed, still holding the gun, my heart pounding. Someone was in the room. I couldn't see anyone, but there was one place I hadn't looked. Under the bed. Saying a quiet prayer for my knees, I crouched down and jumped as close to the door as I could. I rushed a few more steps towards the light switch and flicked it on. After quickly scanning the room, I pointed the gun toward the bed and waited, listening for any movement. When none came, I took a deep breath and slowly kneeled down close to the bed, flipping the comforter up and looking underneath.

I scanned the area. A small lump was near the foot of the bed. I pulled it out and immediately dropped it, gasping and backing away.

Someone had been in my room.

I walked to the adjoining door, opened it, and knocked on the door that led to Brady's room. He opened the door.

"What's wrong?"

"This was under my bed," I said. Holding up the doll.

Brady shook off sleep and said, "Is that a voodoo doll?"

"That is exactly what it is. Someone's playing a game with me," I said, tossed the figure on the end table near the bed.

"Where did you find it?" Brady asked.

"Under the bed," I said. Doing my best to sound relaxed, but I was nervous. Someone had been in my room.

"Okay, you're not sleeping in there again. I'll sleep on the little couch. You can take the bed. Also, we need to find out more about the curse story. This is really strange. Let's ask around and see what we can find out." Brady said.

I hated to admit it, but Brady was right.

"Fine. We're going down the rabbit hole."

"I think we could also ask Holden about it. He seemed to be fond of the family. I bet he knows about this."

It was a good idea. Holden was connected, and he might even know something about the tale himself.

"I'm leery about reaching out to Holden because he might tell Grayson that we're meeting. I didn't like how he just showed up when I was talking with Darcy."

"That is odd, but Darcy might have a different relationship with Grayson. Holden was more than happy to help us. Remember, he snuck us into the office to get pictures of the calendar."

"True. I'll reach out and see if he'll meet with us again."

I sent Holden a message just after eight asking to meet.

Instead of typing out a response, Holden's number came across the screen of my phone.

"Holden. Thanks for—"

"I have information about where Nathan was before he went to the Bayou Sauvage."

"Great. Where was he?"

Silence filled the phone. I used the moment to ask, "Hey, while I have you on the line, do you know of any ghost stories or curses that are supposed to be connected to the Broussards?"

Holden remained silent.

"Are you there?" I asked.

"Yes, I'm here. I had hoped we wouldn't have to talk about this. It's an old tale that has nothing to do with reality, but I think someone is using the old story to throw a paranormal twist on things."

"I found a something under my room."

"What? In your hotel room?"

"Yes. Under the bed."

Holden sighed. "Okay. None of this is true, but I'll tell you the story. A man named Moses escaped from the Broussard plantation and moved into the swamps. When he went back to get his family, he was shot by Ellis Broussard, one of Nathan's forefathers. Moses' wife was so heartbroken that she decided to take a revenge that would last for generations to come."

"What are the details of this curse?"

Holden sighed. "This is silly and I'm sure it doesn't have anything to do with the doll you found. Why do you want to know about mythology?"

"Someone could be using the story. I just want to be familiar with it."

"Alright. The story claims that the wife took some of Ellis Broussard's hair, dipped it into blood, and buried it out near the swamps. Allegedly, she cursed the Broussards and said they would lose the youngest son for all future generations. The youngest son would die before his thirty-fifth birthday."

"Nathan was already thirty-five."

"Right. That's why this is just a story."

"Is it true that several Broussards in the past have died before thirty-five?"

"Yes, but it's easy to die. The Broussards have always had a lot of money, and the boys had freedom. They went on safaris, or partying on the wrong side of town. Nathan was brave. He was challenging big oil, which is rare, and he was a politician. I'm sure there were plenty of people in the shadows that were upset by things Nathan did. It's just not that hard for life to end."

Holden was right. Life was precious and could be fleeting.

"Thank you for sharing. I just wanted to know the story."

"Well, there might be more to it. Not in the spooky sense, but someone may be able to tell you something about the last few hours of Nathan's life. He's probably the last person who saw him alive."

"Who is it?"

"Nathan's old science teacher, Mr. Buford. He lives near the refuge. Nathan was very active in the New Orleans East. He really cared about that community and wanted to make it better. Mr. Buford is probably well into his eighties now, but you'll catch him out every day doing yardwork, looking out for neighbors, taking a walk, and enjoying life. Sometimes, he'll take the boat out on the lake, but other times, he just sits on his porch and has a bourbon. He and Nathan used to do that a lot. I've been there a few times with him."

"Do you think Mr. Buford would talk with me?"

"Oh yeah. He's heartbroken that Nathan is gone."

"Did Nathan do anything else in that area?"

"The Bayou Sauvage is really the only thing over there that you would go to. Nathan's father helped get the measure passed that created the national refuge, so it's special to him. Some businesses have opened around there, but the area was hit pretty hard by Katrina, and it hasn't recovered. But Nathan believed in it. He thought that if we could just get some opportunities in that area, the violence would decrease. It's really sad that he's gone. Those people are going to miss him."

20

———

Holden called Mr. Buford and got the okay for Brady and me to stop by his place. Before we left, I switched my screensaver to a ten minute delay and closed all the tabs.

"What are you doing?" Brady asked. Standing behind me.

"I'm setting a trap for the creeper that keeps coming into my room."

"Why if it's not human?"

"I guess nothing will happen. A supernatural being probably doesn't need a computer."

Mr. Buford's house was about fifteen minutes from Bayou Sauvage. We pulled up in front of the small bungalow with a beautiful, red, antique truck parked in the driveway.

Bobby Buford was around six foot five, with fuzzy white and gray hair along the side of his head, and a shiny bald top. His skin was dark and smooth, and his movements were calculated and slow. The old man was digging around in a flower bed when we showed up.

"Mr. Buford?"

"Yes?" he looked up. "Do I know you?" Mr. Buford stood and adjusted his coke-bottle glasses.

"No. My name is Sylvia Wilcox, and I was wondering if we could ask you a few questions. We've heard that you were close to Mr. Nathan Broussard."

"He was a good man. Such a shame to lose someone like that. It's all everybody is talking about. Nathan Broussard was special, and he did a lot in this community."

"It sounds like Nathan was a great person. We're truly sorry for your loss. I've been told that he used to come and drink a bourbon with you now and then."

"That's true, but the talks on this porch are private. What gentlemen talk about in private stays between those gentlemen."

"Understood. I totally respect that sentiment. But sir, one of those gentlemen was brutally murdered and I think he deserves justice, and since he was your friend, I know you do, too."

Mr. Buford nodded his head and said, "Booby Buford. Who are you two?"

"I am Sylvia Wilcox," I said. "and this is—"

"Brady Kepler. Sir, is that your 1940 Ford Pickup in the drive?"

Mr. Buford removed his glasses. "Son, you are one in a million. No one knows the year that truck was made. I'm so impressed."

"I'm a mechanic, so it's actually not too impressive. I love vehicles."

"Well, now I feel like I've got something in common with you. Also, Holden told me some people were coming by, but I had to check and make sure you two were who he was talking about. Another guy came by trying to ask questions the other day. He was real pushy."

"Do you know his name?"

"Nope. Like I said. He was pushy, so I told him to get on out of here and not come back. Ya'll come on up on the porch and we'll see what we can figure out about the questions ya'll have," Mr. Buford said.

Brady's truck knowledge had put a little extra pep in Mr. Buford's step. We followed him onto the porch, which spanned the entire front of the house. Two end tables and four large rocking chairs were lined up on both sides of the door. Brady and I took seats.

"Y'all want some sweet tea or something?" Mr. Buford asked.

"I think we're okay. We don't want to take up too much of your time."

"Okay, well, I'll tell you what I know," Mr. Buford said, easing into one of the rocking chairs.

"Nathan came by here New Year's Eve. It was late afternoon. He sat on the porch with me, had a bourbon—nothing out of the ordinary. We talked about his campaign and his family. He told me his kids were out to a sleepover at his brother's house, so I said to him, 'You and Krista are going to enjoy a nice quiet evening watching the fireworks from the balcony?' He just smiled, so I didn't push any further."

"What time was Nathan here, Mr. Buford?" Brady asked.

"Oh man, he must've been here maybe two-ish, almost three. He usually stopped by here when he had something heavy on his mind, but he didn't really want to talk about it. He said he likes to come here because he doesn't have to talk about things. There were times, as a politician, that he had to talk about things even if he was angry or sad, and even if he just wanted to be left alone. So, when he came here, I never forced anything out of him."

"Makes sense. How did you and Nathan become friends?"

"I was his science teacher in high school. Nathan's parents didn't send him and his brother to any prestigious school or anything like that. They didn't think that was a way for their boys because they already had a future set out for them. This kept Nathan humble. They knew they had oil to fall back on. There was no need for college, but Nathan loved to learn. He enjoyed science and school in general, so he used to help me out in science lab. Very curious young man. After he graduated, he headed to college and went on to law school. He did his thing. I was really proud of him. So was his dad, but Mrs. Broussard wasn't pleased that Nathan wasn't terribly religious. He went to church when he had to, but mostly he was focused on getting into office."

"So, Nathan's mother wasn't into the political scene?" Brady asked.

"That's right, son. She was a lot like Krista, Nathan's wife. They think little of the profession. I was surprised when he got married so young, but that was a shotgun wedding. He made good on it. He took care of his family, and he loved his wife and kids. Somebody, probably politically motivated, didn't like that, and they killed a good man. End of story."

"Somebody like that deserves justice, Mr. Buford. It's not the end of the story. It's just the beginning," I countered.

"Well now, I see you got some fire. What do you want to know? How can I help you solve this murder?"

"What can you tell us about the curse placed on the Broussards?" Brady asked.

"Brady. We—"

"Hold on. Don't admonish him, young lady. Now you've got my attention. If you're looking into anything with the Broussards, you need to know about this. First, the story is probably true. At least the part about Moses escaping, going back for his family, and being killed. It's also probably true that his beloved put a curse on the family."

"But curses don't exist," I said.

"I guess it depends on what you think is going on. Here's

something you probably don't know. Mrs. Broussard is very religious, but also very superstitious. Do you know that very few people know about Nathan's real birthday?"

"His mother didn't want to take any chances," Brady said. "See, Sylvia. This is something we need to hear about."

"That's right, young man. Now, if you ask around, people will tell you it's because she thought someone would use the information to their advantage, but I think there's more to it. I'm not a believer in the otherworldly stuff, but there are things we can't explain."

"Yes. Some events are beyond our comprehension. Do you have any other theories about what happened to Nathan?" I asked, hoping to get something more concrete.

"Nathan had seventy-five percent control of the family business."

"Leaving the brother with twenty-five percent," Brady said. "That's got to sting."

Mr. Buford peered over the top of his glasses. "Kind of sounds like a motive, doesn't it?"

"It does, but who gets the money now that Nathan is gone? Does it go to the wife, or will Grayson get more power and a larger cut now?" I asked.

"That's kind of trick question. The way I understand it, and things could have changed by now, Grayson will not get full control. In fact, Nathan told me a while back that he thinks his mother will have the seventy-five percent control of the company passed down to his son, and a custodian will be put in charge of the children's portion."

"Let me guess. Krista doesn't know any of this," I said.

"The part about Grayson not having much control is common knowledge. He has a reputation that hasn't faded even though he's trying to be this holy roller now. The wife, though, I doubt she knows about the way things are set up in the will."

"How do you know so much about what the Broussards have set up in the will?" I asked.

"It's in a trust. I was one of the witnesses. Like I said, things may have changed."

"You think Grayson killed Nathan?" Brady asked.

Mr. Buford shrugged his shoulders. "Grayson was the wild child and their daddy hated that. He made sure that Nathan was in control of the company, and he wanted the company to go through that side of the family. Over the past few years, Grayson has had a bunch of businesses that have failed, and now he's got this church. He's hungry for money and willing to do anything to get it."

"That makes sense if the Broussards helped Holden get out of trouble," I said.

"Yes, but there's more. I think Holden has turned things around, but have you talked with the parents of the kid he killed?" Mr. Buford asked.

"No," I said. Brady and I looked at each one another.

"They have some interesting tales about the Timmons boy. Get in touch with them. They'll be happy to tell you about what they've experienced."

WE TALKED with Mr. Buford for a few more minutes before heading back to the hotel. As I pushed the door open, I was sure someone had been in my room.

"Look," I said. Pointing at the laptop on the bed.

"What?"

"It's been moved."

"Are you sure?" Brady asked.

"Yes."

"Grab the laptop and let's go to my room."

Brady put his hand on the small of my back and gently led me to his room.

"Do you think that weird Lucian guy has someone sneaking into your room?"

"I don't know, but someone is things I have something important," I said.

"LET'S wrap this thing up and get out of here," Brady said, folding his arms.

"Yes. We need to get enough evidence to get Madalyn out of jail and then we're gone."

"Okay. Let's talk about what Mr. Buford told us. If Grayson is Mrs. Broussard's favorite, why wouldn't she change the will?" Brady asked.

"Respect. Maybe she doesn't want to go against her husband's wishes. The money, after all, is from his lineage."

"Good point. Why would Krista lie about the will?"

"No idea about that. Let's get caught up on what's happening with the investigation," I said, opening my laptop. Brady turned on the television. The news of Nathan's murder had shocked the state. Every channel was running updates that she also lied about being kidnapped. If she's telling the police she's been abducted after telling us she was hiding out because she was scared, I think she has to be pretty high on the suspect list. Clearly, she has something to hide.

"Krista Broussard tells a harrowing story of how she was abducted by a man and a woman— criminal tag team that tried to extort her for money and threatened to murder her, just like her husband.'

"The police are looking for a black woman, short with a medium build, and a white man with long, blonde hair and a long beard. The man is said to be of medium height and thin."

Brady and I looked at one another.

"She didn't just... Describe us. Did she?" Brady said.

I shook my head. "Unfortunately, yes. She just described us. Krista set us up."

"Also tonight, we're shocked to report that the woman who was arrested in connection with Nathan Broussard's murder has been released on bond. She is not allowed to leave the parish and must wear an ankle monitor."

"Madalyn's out?" Brady said. His eyes were wide with shock.

"I can't believe it. I guess this Paschal Oliver guy really found a bang-up lawyer. We need to talk with her asap."

"Are you sure it's safe for us to be here? We basically were just implicated in an abduction."

It was a problem. All Krista had to do was tell the police it was us. They would surely believe her.

"We have to move fast."

I called Paschal. His phone went to voicemail. I tried Carson next, but he didn't pick up either.

"Both the lawyer and Carson know we're trying to help Madalyn. Why would we have to hear that Madalyn is out on bail through the news?"

Brady folded his arms.

"Well, technically, there are additional suspects now. The same people that kidnapped Krista might also have killed her husband."

"Good point. I can't believe that Krista set us up that way."

My phone rang. A local number appeared on the screen.

"No idea who this is, but it's local," I said before answering.

"Where are you?" A whispered filled the phone.

"Madalyn? Oh, my gosh. What happened in Sauvage Bayou?"

"You and Brady need to leave town as soon as possible."

"Where are you?"

Madalyn was quiet for a moment before saying, "Get out while you can."

21

____

I wasn't sure what to make of Madalyn's phone call. After filling Brady in, he said. "Well, I guess we can't count on Madalyn to help us solve this thing."

"That's bad news because I have no idea what is going on here. We've got an oilman, a brother that needs and wants money, and a wife who just lied about being kidnapped. Any of them could be guilty."

"So, what do we do now?" Brady asked.

"We find out who killed Nathan Broussard. Let's check in with Martin and see if he has anything new."

Martin had some interesting tidbits for us.

"According to Kara, and Madalyn is out on bail. She has to wear an ankle monitor, and she's stashed away in the Garden District of the city."

"Wow. Okay. What else do you know?"

"Kara is not happy about the secrecy of between her mom and Carson, so she dug into things and found out what's going on. Kara discovered that her mother has a lot of secrets and she's mad. So, like any disgruntled adult child, Kara was ready to talk."

"That's great because I do not know what's going on with Madalyn. I can't reach anyone involved in the case. Madalyn called, but she just told me to get out of town while I can."

"Sounds like good advice."

"Maybe, but I'm committed now. I will leave when I know Madalyn is off the hook."

"I thought you might say that. Listen, I'm getting worried about you. If you guys don't get this solved soon, I'm heading there to wrap this thing up. You two are in real danger."

"Okay. We'll work fast," I said. "Gotta go."

"I found some things about the kid Holden killed," Brady said after I hung up with Martin.

"Yeah? What's the story?"

"Dean Becker was the only child of May and Justin Becker. It's one of those sad stories where the parents struggled to have a child and after they got their miracle, a sucker punch took his life."

"That's devastating."

"Yep. The parents have set up a charity in the boy's honor." Brady handed me his phone.

A tall and lanky boy with a shy smile filled the screen. Large shoulder bones poked through a white t-shirt in the picture that headlined the website.

"He was so thin," I said.

"Yeah. A sucker punch would have caused him to fall hard."

The charity was for teens that had severe scoliosis. Dean had suffered from the condition as a child and had undergone a major surgery to straighten his back. His freckled filled cheeks and braces made him look like an overgrown preteen, but the caption of the picture said the photo was from his senior pictures.

"The parents might be worth contacting," Brady said.

"Mr. Buford said they had a story to tell."

MAY and Justin Becker were eager to speak with me.

"We've been waiting for someone to look into this kid since we lost Dean. During the trial, he was untouchable. We've always thought there was more to it than what we were told," May Becker told me.

After explaining who I was, and why I was calling, May invited us to their home.

The next morning, we drove to the Becker home in Mandeville, Louisiana. The cottage sat back from the road. Sitting on at least an acre, the house was located in a neighborhood where each house had a decent amount of land, providing privacy.

A woman with short spiked brown hair was standing on the porch, waving. Her face was solemn and still. Brady and I returned the wave. The woman climbed down the front stairs of the house, her legs long and angular like the pictures of her son on the website.

"Justin is preparing. This is hard for us, but we must do it. May Becker," she said, stretching her arm out for a handshake.

"Thank you for taking the time to talk with us. This is Brady Kepler, and I'm Sylvia Wilcox. Pleasure to meet you."

We shook hands all around, and May motioned for us to follow her.

"Losing Dean is the only thing keeping us going these days, so we're always ready to talk to anyone who speaks his name."

"We appreciate that. We'll be as quick as soon as possible," I said.

May turned around as we reached the front door.

"Please take as long as you need. We're never tired of talking about our boy."

The cottage had an open concept layout. We stepped into

the living room, where Justin Becker was standing near the couch with his arms folded. Both May and Justin were over six feet and thin. Justin's blonde hair was cut close, but also spiked. He nodded and paced after May closed the door.

"What do you want to know?" Justin asked.

"Slow down, honey," May said, walking over and gently touching Justin's arm.

"Okay. I just don't know..."

Brady and I turned away, giving the couple what little privacy their small living room offered. Regret welled in my throat. I hated re-opening a wound that could never truly heal.

"Can I get you two anything?" May asked after calming Justin.

"No ma'am. We are fine," Brady said.

"Let's start again. I'm Justin, and you've already met my wife, May. We're happy to help bring justice in this case, even though Mr. Broussard prevented us from getting closure and justice for our son."

"Thank you, Mr. Becker. I'm Sylvia and this is Brady. We are looking into the murder of Nathan Broussard," I said.

"You want to know if I killed him? The answer is no, but I think Holden Timmons is a good suspect. He's already killed once and gotten away with it. I don't know all the facts, but he's got a temper and a checkered past."

"He had major problems back in middle school. And while we know that Dean's death was accidental, Holden should have been held accountable."

"What happened at the trial?"

"Basically, the Broussards stepped in to help Holden, and the next thing we knew, it went from manslaughter with the possibility of two to five years in jail to a year of probation. The lawyer was high priced and skilled, but the prosecutor also seemed to be Team Holden. She kept bringing up his age and called him a boy several times. It would have made anyone feel sorry for him," May said.

"Do you know how the Broussards came to know Holden?" I asked.

Justin's brow furrowed, and he paced while he spoke. "Grayson Broussard was working with young men before he became a pastor. The guy has always been the screw up of the family, but this seemed to fit. He was running a nonprofit that worked with young men who had gotten into trouble at school or had done time at juvie. Like I said, Holden had problems in middle school. It was rumored that he used to hurt animals, which is a huge red flag. He was also caught with drugs in the eighth grade, so, of course, we didn't encourage Dean to hang out with him," Justin said.

"That's understandable. How did Justin and Dean end up becoming friends?"

"I wouldn't say they were friends. The two ended up coming into contact when they both joined the basketball team in tenth grade. By that time, Holden seemed to be turning things around. Part of that was probably due to the fishing trips and character-building classes he was taking at Grayson Broussard's nonprofit. We weren't thrilled to see Dean and Holden together, but we thought the kid was doing better, so we let it go. Huge mistake."

"So, Grayson Broussard had a nonprofit to help children before the church?"

"Yes."

"How long was Grayson running the nonprofit?"

"No idea," Justin said. "The guy jumps around from one thing to another. His brother was the stable, upstanding citizen. That's why we were so shocked when he stepped in and helped Holden. I'd always had respect for Nathan Broussard. We couldn't believe he was inserting himself in the trial."

"We even contacted his office and asked to speak with him," May said, throwing her hands up in frustration.

"Did he speak with you?" I asked.

"Yes, but he didn't answer our questions. We asked why he was involved at all. He even mentioned Holden at some of his campaign rallies. It was weird because Nathan Broussard wasn't known to be soft on crime," May said.

"Are the Timmons politically connected?" Brady asked.

"No. I think Grayson just took Holden under his wing. He needed a young man who would do his bidding. We've heard that Holden is one of the main recruiters for Grayson Broussard's church and he worked for Nathan Broussard's campaign. Obviously, we don't know everything about what goes on behind the scenes, but I think Holden sold his soul for the assistance they provided him during the trial. The fact that Grayson is running in his dead brother's spot is sick. The man was murdered. Why not take time to mourn your brother? But no. The Broussards want money and power. It's all they care about, and Holden Timmons is their puppet. He's now Grayson's number one campaign aide."

"Maybe the Timmons have something on the Broussards," Brady suggested.

"The two families don't seem to be from the same world. Something is bringing them together," I added.

"We agree, but so far, we have no idea what that something is," Justin said. "Chuck Timmons worked for the Broussards at some point, but hundreds of people work for the Broussards." Justin said. "The Timmons kid was also just one of several kids that went through Grayson Broussard's program. We don't understand why he's special."

"It just feels like bad luck. Like Justin said, Dean wasn't even really friends with Holden. They were out on Sauvage Bayou, which is strange because that's very close to where Nathan Broussard was killed. The boys were out on Grayson Broussard's boat. We don't know exactly what happened, but Holden says they were just out fishing. Dean had told us he was going to dinner with the basketball team, but that turned out to be a lie. He knew we never would have agreed to him going out on a boat with Holden Timmons."

22

"Why would Grayson, a grown man, lend his boat to a boy he knew was troubled?" Brady asked.

We were driving back to the hotel. Most of the ride was silent. The Becker's had given us a lot of food for thought.

"The Beckers put a whole new spin on things. Holden has been our little helper—getting Nathan's schedule for us and reaching out to see if we need anything, but his intentions might not be as honest as they seem."

"He seems eager."

"But so did the Becker's. I wasn't expecting that at all. I guess—" I stopped mid-sentence.

"What is it?" Brady asked.

"Holden knew about the doll under my bed. I told him something was left in my room and he said that the story about the Broussard curse was silly and he was sure it didn't have anything to do with the doll I found."

"Holden Timmons was in your room."

"He doesn't want us digging any deeper. The doll was meant to scare us off." I said.

"Did Darcy confirm Holden's whereabouts?"

"No. She couldn't confirm the time that she or Holden arrived at the party. After several drinks she was out of the count, so her recollections don't exonerate Holden."

"And while Nathan seems to really like Nathan, he is more enamored with Grayson." Brady said.

"The Beckers and Mr. Buford seem to think Holden would do anything to make Grayson happy. I wasn't thinking of Holden as a suspect before, but now that we've talked with them, he seems like a viable candidate."

My phone rang as soon as we pulled into the parking lot of the hotel. I fished it out of my purse and answered. Before I could greet the person on the other end, Grayson Broussard said, "Can you meet me at my cabin by Bayou Sauvage?"

"Mr. Brousard?"

"Ms. Sylvia, please call me Grayson."

He purred into the phone. His voice was calm and smooth.

"Any particular reason why you'd like to meet?"

I motioned for Brady to lean over so he could hear what Grayson had to say.

"I've discovered something that might be useful to your investigation. The bayou is a special place for my family, so we've always kept a cabin close by. I'd love to show you some of our southern hospitality, but I also think what I have to say will fix what we're going through. The cabin seems like a fitting place to meet and talk."

Brady shook his head. I nodded and said, "Okay. What time?"

"As soon as possible. I'm already here."

"Send me directions and I will be there," I said. Brady was shaking his head.

"Sylvia, this is not a good idea," Brady said.

"He wants me on his territory. I think that's the only way I'm going to get anything from him. After that visit with the Becker's, I think Grayson is the key to solving this case."

"But we can't rule him out as a suspect. He might be dangerous."

"You're right, but I need to talk to him. I'll take my gun."

"You don't know what you're walking into," Brady said.

The directions to Grayson's cabin popped up on the screen of my phone. I read over them.

"Sylvia, this isn't good. You need—"

I held up my hand. "Settle down. Maybe you can come with me. Just sit in the car and be on the lookout for Grayson carrying my body out to the lake."

"Not funny. Okay. That's a better plan."

GRAYSON'S CABIN was small and unassuming. It sat precariously close to the water with a view out over the Rigolets. Perched on stilts, the cabin had two boat slips, an outdoor dining area situated around a small pond, and was surrounded by palm trees. Grayson was standing out front, his hand shoved in his pockets. He continued to stare out over the water until I was a few feet away.

"You brought someone with you? Is there someone in the car?"

"Yes," I said, deliberately not elaborating.

"Want to bring him up? I've got sweet tea, crackers, and cheese."

"No. He's fine in the car. What did you want to talk about?"

"Ms. Sylvia, have you ever seen such a beautiful sunset? Do they have things this wonderful up north in your neck of the woods?"

"Michigan is mostly rural, unspoiled land. Most of the people live in the bottom of the state and I'm sure we can agree on the fact that its people that ruin things. And yes, we have great beauty."

Grayson nodded. "A defender of her homeland. I like that. I feel the same way about this place. I will fight to the death to keep her safe. That is why I'm running in my brother's place. I know what needs to be done."

The long build up to whatever it was Grayson had to tell me was getting annoying. I decided to cut to the chase.

"Who killed your brother?"

"Well, the cops say it's this strange woman from your part of town, but now they've let her out on bail, so I wonder if this is a case of botched police work again. There's a lot of federal oversight of the police department. It makes it hard to do that job."

"The Consent Decree."

Grayson took his hands out of his pockets, folded his arms, and tilted his head.

"You know about the decree?"

"I do. I also know that any type of federal oversight over complicates things and makes a cop's life difficult. The paperwork becomes a priority and crimes go unsolved."

"That's why I've been looking into things on my own. I know you've been doing the same, but that's what I want to talk with you about. I hope you don't mind, but I invited a friend to help us figure this out." Grayson's lips curled into a sinister smile.

I glanced back at the driveway. An abnormally tall, pale man made his way towards us. His stride was confident and bold. I saw the shine of his perfect teeth before his sharp aquiline features came into view.

"Ms. Sylvia. We meet again," Lucian said, holding out his hand.

I ignored Lucian and turned back to Grayson.

"What is he doing here?" I asked.

"We didn't want to bring this up to you because we figured

it really had nothing to do with Nathan's death but at this point, it seems that you're rather enchanted with everything morsel of our lives, so we've decided to tell you the truth," Lucian said

"Lucian and I have a deal that's been in the works for months. Nathan was not a fan. He didn't want us to move forward with it but it's the best thing for the area, and for both of our companies. Obviously, now that my brother is gone, I have to do what's best for my beloved state. But some people might not understand the full vision. That's why we want to ask you to leave things as they are and go back to where you came from. I'm sure someone there misses you."

My heart thumped against my chest. Grayson had betrayed his brother to work with Lucian.

"Is that why Nathan is dead now?"

"No, it's nothing like that. He just wasn't on board. There was nothing that we could do to change his mind, but this is what has to happen. Yes, the world will move on from fossil fuels at some point, but it won't be for a long time. Not in our lifetimes. So meanwhile, we might as well capitalize on the opportunity and help others make a living from this great industry," Grayson said.

I shook my head. I should've been shocked, but I wasn't. Grayson was a pastor, and even though I had learned long ago that many men of the cloth were dishonest and could not be trusted, I still felt a tinge of shock when I heard about it.

"Is it because your church is failing?" I asked.

"That's a lie. My church is not failing. Do we need to work on some things? Sure. But we are doing just fine."

"You don't understand, Ms. Sylvia. This is business and you are not a businessperson. So, I advise that you pack a little bag and go back to that big old Victorian like I told you and you just settle in, get you some cats, and live out your life," Lucian said.

Anger filled my throat. I felt absolutely betrayed that

Grayson had not told me that Lucian would be at this meeting. I was terribly uncomfortable. I did not like this man at all.

"Excellent. Well, I bet the police would be interested in hearing that the two of you had a big deal that wasn't going to happen until Nathan was murdered. Why don't we just turn over all this information to the police and let them figure it out, then?"

Lucian laughed. "See, that's the trouble with you. You don't understand; it's not for the police to figure out and the police don't care about any of this. The only person who is poking around and disturbing things is you."

"That's because an innocent man is dead and someone I care about is being blamed for it. She did not kill anyone. Now, if you can clear that up, I'll be on the next flight back to Michigan."

Lucian came over and stood too close to me and stared into my eyes. I didn't flitch but my heart was racing. Locking eyes with him caused a shiver to run through my body.

"Here's the way the world works. When something happens, someone must be held responsible for it. Sometimes, the responsible party is the person that caused the issue. Other times, it's the person that unfortunately takes the fall. Learn a lesson from your friend. She stumbled into the wrong place at the wrong time, and she had twenty thousand dollars on her. She was in the water with a dead body. You and I both know that's enough information for them to prosecute and convict. Sadly, she's probably not guilty, but you know that doesn't matter. I'd hate to see something like that happen to you," Lucian said, winking at me.

"A case can turn quickly," I said.

"You're right. But you know, Ms. Sylvia, in this life, it doesn't always matter what really happened. What matters is what you see," Grayson said.

"No. What matters is what you can prove and there is no proof that Madalyn is the person that killed Nathan."

Lucian threw his head back and laughed. "See, that's where we differ. Madalyn Price was seen with the body right after Nathan was killed. Why is it that no one else was around from what we can see? So, that means she's got to pay the price, even if somebody else was responsible. That's how things work in the real world."

"If this Madalyn woman didn't kill my brother, then who did?" Grayson said. Raising his voice and working hard to sound frustrated.

"I'm surprised you don't have anyone in mind."

"What do you mean?"

"You have a congregation of people who worship you. I'm sure someone, especially one of the young and impressionable members, would be eager to do your bidding."

"She thinks you're a king," Lucian said.

"Those that walk without the light think in such sinister ways. Ms. Sylvia, I work to bring joy and happiness to the faithful. You come to church this Sunday. Join us for the altar call. It will change your life."

"I think I'll pass. I don't want that kind of change in my life."

"Just go home, Ms. Sylvia," Lucian said. "I'll make sure you regret it if you don't."

I turned my back to Lucian.

"Is that all?" I asked Grayson.

"Yes ma'am."

"Okay. Thanks. I'll see myself out."

"Wait. I've got something you might want to see. You might consider it the main event," Grayson said.

Lucian nodded his head and chuckled. My heart raced. *You've got protection,* I reminded myself.

Grayson sauntered over to the big screen television on the wall beside the bar area, grabbed the remote, and turned it on. I gasped as soon as I saw Madalyn enter the frame. She was wearing the outfit she'd had on the day we arrived in New Orleans, smiling, and talking with Grayson. There wasn't any sound, so I had no idea what she was saying, but her face was animated, her arms flailing in the air with glee. What was happening in the video?

Lucian entered the frame. His arms were crossed until Madalyn turned around. The two shook hands and exchanged words before Grayson came and stood beside them. The three formed a circle, chatted for a short while, and shook hands. Had they paid Madalyn to kill Nathan? I realized I was holding my breath in anticipation of the explanation, but all that came was loud laughter from both Grayson and Lucian.

"This might not be what you thought, huh?" Lucian said.

I didn't want to show my hand, but I was absolutely shocked. What had Madalyn been doing with Grayson and Lucian? Was she actually the killer? She'd just been released on bond.

"Oh, I bet you're wondering if Madalyn is the killer. Well, what do you think? Grayson, cue up the next clip," Lucian said.

Grayson flipped to another video. This one was a shaking cellphone clip of Madalyn leaving jail and getting into a gray Jaguar. The camera flipped around. Lucian smiled and shook his head before waving and stopping the video.

"Ms. Sylvia. What do you think of that?" Grayson asked as he turned off the television.

I considered a response. What could I say? Working hard to stay calm, I waited a moment before saying, "I'll see myself out."

23

———————

Brady was leaning against the car when I rushed back to the parking area.

"Everything okay?" Brady asked.

"Let's go," I said, climbing into the passenger seat. Brady hopped in and started the car.

"What happened?"

"Lucian was there."

"Really? Oh, man. I know you can't stand that guy. Why was he there?"

"They wanted to show me a video of them talking with Madalyn."

"Madalyn? She knows them?"

"Looked like she was pretty comfortable with them."

"What do you think is going on?" Brady asked.

I leaned my head against the edge of the door. "I have no idea. Let's just go back to the hotel and regroup. Should we even be trying to help Madalyn? Is she the killer? I have no idea. Just another person we can't trust."

"Seriously, what's going on here? I feel like everyone is against us. What do you make of Madalyn being with Grayson and Lucian?"

"No idea. But I guess if she knew Nathan, it's not too odd that she knew his brother. The part that is just inconceivable is Lucian getting Madalyn out of jail. It was so disturbing. I don't know where to start."

I was tired of running around in circles.

"Maybe we should just pack our bags and go back to our respective homes."

"Hey. We're not giving up. We can figure this out," Brady said, parking in front of our rooms.

"I certainly hope so. Maybe I've lost..." I stopped mid-sentence. The door to my room was cracked.

"What are you staring at?"

"The door. It's open. Stay here," I said, getting out of the car.

Brady followed close behind, ignoring my recommendation that he stay in the car. I ran my hand over the butt of my gun and stood still at the door, listening. I heard the creak of a door. It sounded like the person was headed into Brady's room through the adjoining door. I nodded my head toward the outside door of Brady's room and pulled out my gun, holding it out in front of myself, gently pushing the door open just wide enough for me to inch into the room. The adjoining door was open. I could hear rustling in Brady's room. I moved slowly, hoping I could catch the perp on the far side of the room. The beam of a flashlight broke the darkness. I could hear rustling near the bathroom, on the opposite side of the room. I pushed the second adjoining door wide open and said, "Do not move."

The figure stopped, but I couldn't make out who the person was.

"Brady," I yelled.

"Yeah?"

"Come in and turn on the light."

I kept the gun focused on the dark shape in the corner of

the room. Brady flipped the light switch. I blinked several times. Barely able to understand what I was seeing.

"It's not what it looks like," Madalyn said, her hands up in the air.

~

"I'M DONE with the games. You need to tell us exactly what is going on. Start off with what you were doing paling around with Grayson Broussard and Lucian," I said.

"I know you think I'm keeping secrets—"

"No more, Madalyn! We have been searching for a way to get the murder charge against you dropped, and we've been working to save your life."

"Madalyn, you know how this goes. We can only help you if we have the truth. Now, what is the truth? What were you doing in the bayou with Nathan?"

"Okay. This is a long story."

"We have time," Brady said.

"Nathan and I met by chance at a fundraising event at a women's shelter. He was curious about me because I was from out of town and seemed to be very involved. Initially, I was cagey with him, but in time, he found out that I'd been helping women get out of abusive situations. Nathan was also passionate about empowering women to get out of terrible relationships. So, we started working together."

"But you were also helping Krista escape her marriage with Nathan, right?" Brady said.

Madalyn nodded. "Yes, and no. She came to me and said Nathan was abusing her. I didn't think it was true, but you never know. It's hard for me to doubt someone when they tell me they're being abused. So, I played it close. See if Nathan was actually mistreating her."

"And what did you find out?" I asked.

"Krista just wanted to leave. I think she felt trapped by Nathan's position and their children. She lied to me."

"Why were you meeting Nathan at the bayou the day he died?"

"So, this is where Lucian and Grayson come into play. When you work with someone who you know can keep secrets, you trust them. And Nathan, because of his position and the fact that he runs a multi-million-dollar company, made it hard for him to trust people. He thought his brother was trying to broker a deal with Lucian behind his back. He asked me to see if I could get information on what they were planning."

"And you can never resist a clandestine situation," I said.

Madalyn shrugged her shoulders. "Guilty. I was intrigued, but I also wanted to help Nathan. He was such a great guy."

"Was it more than just working together between you two?" Brady asked.

"No. Nathan was a friend. We shared information about our relationships and troubles. There was an attraction between us, but we kept it professional."

"What was the endgame with Grayson and Lucian? You looked very comfortable with them."

"I went to Grayson's church for a talk Lucian was giving. He was trying to get the community on board so that the people would put pressure on Nathan to move forward with the oil rig project. I made myself known and presented myself as a possible investor. They knew I was in town from another state, so they assumed I had some means, and let's just say I pretend well."

"Do you think Grayson killed Nathan?" Brady asked.

Madalyn's brow creased. "I don't know. He's definitely willing to do just about anything for money. But I didn't see who killed Nathan. When I showed up, he was on the shore, but very close to the water. I didn't know what was going on at first. I rushed over to Nathan, he got up, and told me he needed help. He stumbled around a bit, and I tried to hold him up, but he fell into the water and died before I could call an ambulance. I tried to get him out of the water... I was in shock. My mind was racing and all I could think was, *I can't let Nathan drown.* In reality, he was already gone. Even so, I had to get him out of the water. He was a friend. I couldn't just leave him. That's what I was doing when that park employee saw me."

Madalyn swiped at her eyes, and her bottom lip quivered. She'd been closer to Nathan than I'd originally thought.

"Have you told the police all of this?

"Nope. Not a word to them. Carson got me a good lawyer."

"Who do you think killed Nathan?" Brady asked.

"Possibly Krista hired someone. Maybe Grayson got tired of pushing for the oil rig deal and decided to have Nathan killed... There are several ways this could have gone down."

"Who knew the two of you were meeting at the bayou?"

Madalyn titled her head and was quiet for a few minutes.

"No one that I can think of. I didn't tell you and Brady, and Nathan came from the office. No one would have known except for maybe his staff."

"Do you know Holden Timmons?" Brady asked.

Madalyn shook her head. "No. Who is that?"

"It's one of Nathan's campaign aides. He's been helping us with information, but something's off with him."

"Well, he might have known. Nathan told me he'd meet me at Bayou Sauvage after he stopped by a friend's house."

"Mr. Buford," Brady said.

"Yeah. The question is, who knew that Nathan was heading to Mr. Buford and then to Bayou Sauvage? He was followed or someone knew where he was going and waited for him."

"It could have been a number of people. He was a politician, from a wealthy family, and his brother got shafted in the will. His father made sure that Nathan had control and now, according to Nathan, his son will get control. Grayson will still not have a chance to run the company."

"Krista told us that Grayson is the favorite of the mother who is still alive. According to Krista, she's changed the will."

Madalyn shook her head. "No. That's false and Krista knows it. She even told me it didn't matter if she left Nathan because the family passes everything down through the men in the family. It's been like that since the Broussard lineage showed up on these shores."

"Do you know about the curse?" Brady asked.

"Actually, I do. Nathan was a little nervous about it. He told me that his mother was scared that something was going to happen to him, but he'd made it to his thirty-fifth birthday, so he felt like the curse might be a hoax."

"When is his birthday?"

"December 30th. I guess most people think it's earlier in December. Nathan said he always had a party three weeks before his birthday when he was younger. His mother was superstitious about the curse. She didn't want anyone to know the actual day he was born, but the Internet exists, so all that went out the window years ago. What about it?"

"Just curious if maybe someone could be using that as a way to throw people off their scent. If the murder was something more supernatural, some cops might be spooked. The public might give into that sentiment, as well. Like it's a self-fulfilling prophecy that Nathan was murdered," Brady said.

"Great point," I said before turning back to Madalyn. 'What's the story with Carson?"

Madalyn sighed. "That's more complicated. Here's the thing. He doesn't care how I get out of this. That's why I'm here."

"What does that mean?"

"It means that suspicion has been shifted to others... Carson thinks I should take advantage of that."

It took me a moment to comprehend what Madalyn was saying.

"Carson thinks you should let the blame be shifted to the kidnappers Krista told the police about."

Madalyn nodded.

"There are great things about Carson Stark, but there are times when I can see that the apple didn't fall too far from the tree."

Carson and I weren't friends, but I thought he at least wouldn't want to do me harm. Setting Brady and I up for a fall left a bitter taste in my mouth.

"It doesn't really matter what Carson thinks. What are you going to do, Madalyn? How can we get these charges dropped?"

"I don't know just yet. Give me a few days. I promise this will all be over soon."

"Where are you staying?"

"I don't want to tell you guys. It might put you in jeopardy."

24

———————

After Madalyn left, Brady and I were pondering our next move when my phone rang.

"I remembered the name of the boat I saw."

It was Bruce Carpenter from the Bayou Sauvage.

"Excellent. What's the name?" I asked, grabbing a pad of paper and pen from the nightstand.

"Sea Witch."

My fingers froze for moment.

"You're sure?"

"Yeah. Positive."

I thanked Bruce Carpenter for calling and ended the call.

"Grayson Broussard's boat was out on the water the evening Nathan was murdered." I said.

Brady sighed. "The question is, who was on the boat?"

I grabbed my laptop. "Let's double check to see what time the Broussard's started their church party on New Year's Eve."

I pulled up the website of Rise and Aspire Church. Sure enough, the video from the party and service they'd held at the church. I click on the old bulletins to see what time the event started.

"Looks like they started the party at 6:30," I said.

"But was Grayson there from the beginning?"

"Good question. Let's watch some of the video."

The first person entered the frame at six-o-clock. It was Jade, the woman I'd spoken to when I'd visited the church. A few other people showed up minutes later and the crew worked to set out bowls of chips, drinks, and burners for the main cour-ses. The initial guests didn't show up until six-forty. As a crowd slowly accumulated around the food tables, the Broussards were nowhere to be found.

"We're twenty minutes in. I don't see any of the family yet." Brady said.

"Right. If Grayson doesn't show up until seven-ish, he could have killed his brother and headed to the church after that. Looks like I need to have another conversation with Grayson Broussard."

WE DECIDED to turn in for the night and track down Grayson Broussard the next morning. Around five-thirty in the morning, Brady was standing over me, shaking my shoulder.

"Sylvia, wake up. You've gotta see this." Brady was standing on the side of the bed with his phone pushed close to my face.

"What time is it?"

"Seven. You slept in."

I sat up in bed. Brady clicked the play button on the video he had pulled up.

"Krista Broussard is being held by the police. We don't know what charges she's facing, but sources suggest that she may be facing conspiracy to commit murder charges, but we haven't been able to confirm this information yet. Ironically, the woman who was origi-nally arrested in the murder of Nathan Broussard has been released

on bail and it seems that this case is just beginning. We hope to have more answers soon."

The video ended. I swung my legs over the side of the bed. "That was unexpected. I don't know what to make of it. I was betting on Grayson being the killer, but what if Krista and Grayson are involved?"

"I think anything is possible at this point. What about Holden?"

"Well, he'd be the perfect candidate to pull off the murder. He admires Grayson and he would have known Nathan's schedule."

"And he's already taken a life."

"You're right. I think we need to talk to Holden one more time. I have a hunch."

After a short text message exchange, I asked Holden if we could meet. He responded with *Sure! Have you found something to help Pastor Grayson?* Finding it odd that he was focused on Grayson when he didn't seem to be in any danger of going onto the suspect list anytime soon, I typed out; *I think I have something that will absolutely help Pastor Grayson.*

"Holden can't meet us until this evening. Maybe we can catch up with Darcy before that. We didn't get a chance to finish our interview because Grayson showed up."

"What do you think Darcy knows?"

"I think she's covering for Holden. She told me they were at a party together the night Nathan was murdered but she can't remember much because she was too intoxicated."

"Or maybe she just doesn't want to remember."

"Precisely what I'm thinking. She works at the Pastry Peddler. Let's pay her a visit."

We got dressed and headed to the small bakery. The Pastry Peddler was a small shop located in a strip mall just west of the city limits. The kitchen was open for customers to see the food-making process in progress. Darcy was kneading a ball of dough when we showed up. She caught sight of us and stopped kneading. I gave her a friendly smile and waited for her to come out into the lobby. A few minutes later, Darcy emerged from the kitchen, donned in a chef's hat and a black apron with a spattering of flour on it.

"You want to talk to me again?" Darcy muttered, running her hands over her apron.

"Yes. I just have a few more questions if you don't mind."

"Sure," she said. Shrugging her shoulders.

"What time did Holden make it to the party on New Year's Eve?"

Darcy folded her arms and shifted her gaze to the floor. "I told you; I was too drunk to know what was going on."

"Darcy," I said, trying to make eye contact. "This is very important. What time did Holden make it to the party?"

Tears sat on the edges of her eyelids.

"It was late. Real late. He said he got stuck at home doing something for his mom. It was weird because I don't really know the people who were hosting the party. I felt so awkward. That's why I ended up drunk. But even so, Holden loves the Broussards. He'd never do anything to hurt them. Is It true that the lady they arrested is free?"

"Yes. She out on bail and Krista Broussard has been arrested. I don't know what happened Nathan, but it's important that the right person pays for his murder."

"Are you protecting Holden?" Brady asked.

Darcy shook her head. "No. I really don't know what happened. Holden was late to the party, but that doesn't mean anything."

"Of course. Unless he murdered Nathan," I said.

"He wouldn't do that," Darcy said in a quiet voice.

"I need you to think really hard. What time did Holden make it to the party?"

Darcy's eyes filled with tears. "Around seven-thirty," she muttered in a quiet voice.

"Did Nathan tell you and Holden where he was going after he left work on New Year's Eve?"

"He said he was meeting with friends in New Orleans East."

That meant Holden knew the direction Nathan was headed that afternoon.

WE FINISHED up with Darcy and headed for the car. I called and sent text messages to Holden after we left the Pastry Peddler. Each call went straight to voicemail. I slipped the phone back into my pocket and it began to buzz almost immediately. I pulled the phone out of my pocket and recognized the number as Grayson Broussard's.

"Omigosh. It's Grayson Broussard. Again he knows I'm meeting with Darcy," I said. Shaking my head.

I opened the phone and held it to my ear.

"Ms. Wilcox, there have been some unfortunate events surrounding my sister-in-law, but I think the cops have it wrong. I need your help. Can you meet me at the cabin this evening?"

25

"Is Lucian going to be there?" I asked.

"No Ms. Wilcox. I'm so sorry for that. We just don't know what you're after, but I feel like you're sincere. Please accept my apology."

"I'll consider it. But, before I say yes or no, what do you have to say about Krista being arrested?"

"I don't think she did anything to my brother. The police are chasing any lead. They don't know what's going on here. I think that she will get out soon, but that doesn't put us any closer to justice."

"What time tonight?"

"Seven. I promise I'll be alone."

～

AFTER BRADY and I got back to the hotel, Holden sent a text message saying: *Something came up. Can't meet tonight.*

I showed Brady the text message.

"What are the odds that Grayson told Holden he's meeting with me?"

"Odds are very good. This time when we go there, I'll not staying in the car. Give me your gun and I'll wait in the distance."

"Good plan. I could be meeting with a killer. Let's grab some binoculars. I'll give you a sign if something goes wrong."

"Sounds good." Brady said.

We ate and headed out to Grayson's cabin. It was a warm dark night. A gentle breeze blew over me as I climbed out of the car.

"Keep an eye out. You see any trouble, come help me out, okay?" I said before closing the door.

I took my time making my way to the cabin. Not terribly excited to meet with Grayson again, I decided to keep the meeting short and sweet. I'd ask questions, hopefully get answers, and leave.

Grayson was standing outside when I arrived, his hands shoved in his pockets.

"Ms. Wilcox, there have been some unfortunate events surrounding my sister-in-law, but I think the cops have it wrong. I need your help."

"You heard about Krista being arrested?"

"Yes."

"I don't think she did anything to my brother. The police are chasing any lead, but they don't know what's going on here. I think that she will get out soon, but that doesn't put us any closer to justice."

"Agreed. What do you think happened to your brother?"

Grayson walked over to a window and looked out onto the water.

"It's such a beautiful night. Let's head out by the dock."

It wasn't a good idea, but I didn't think Grayson was going to kill me. Besides, Brady was waiting for me. He knew to come and help if something went wrong.

I followed Grayson to the dock.

"Ms. Wilcox, I've been working to help lost souls for a long time. Sometimes people lose their way, but that doesn't mean they aren't worth our time. That's why I have been working with young people for years. I want them all to have a second chance."

"I hear you're close to Holden."

"Oh yeah. He's a good kid."

"So, tell me why he hit Dean Becker."

"That was an accident. The boy was delicate. Holden couldn't have known the boy was going to die."

"But you and Nathan helped get him off for the crime. Why?"

Grayson shook his head. "It was a mistake and the young man was going to lose a portion of his promising future. We had to step in. There is no middle ground," Grayson said, his eyes staring off into the distance. "You're either with the kingdom or you're not."

"Is killing those who aren't considered working for the kingdom on the menu?"

"Yes, at times, but I didn't kill my brother."

"Who makes the decisions to take a life," I asked.

"Sometimes God. Sometimes me. I'm saving souls. You wouldn't understand."

"Grayson, who killed your brother?"

A swift blow to my right shoulder knocked me to the ground. My head hit the inside of my arm, saving me from a concussion, or worse. I gathered myself and rolled onto my back. A Mardi Gras mask greeted me. I inhaled sharply and froze for a moment before rolling out of the person's grasp.

"We'll put her in the water," a man's voice said.

"She doesn't know anything for sure. We can let her live. No one will believe whatever she says," Grayson said, his voice thin.

"She knows enough. No one will question it, pastor. I think it's the only way."

"I'm a man of God—"

"You got me into this. Now you're going to get some blood on your hands," the man in the mask said.

The voice was faintly familiar. I stayed still while the two argued, running the options through my head. Jumping off the deck was a possibility, but I wasn't a powerful swimmer. I could run, but the brackish marsh would be hard to maneuver.

"I can't take a life unless God says it is necessary," Grayson yelled.

I slid slowly toward the edge of the deck. I needed something loud to get Brady's attention. Grayson and the man in the mask were staring at one another in anger. It was no longer clear who the boss was.

"We're on the deck!" I screamed at the top of my lungs before taking a deep breath and throwing myself into the water. I knew the man in the mask would come soon and swam as hard as I could through the murky water. Within minutes, I felt a hand around my ankle. Struggling to kick the hand away, I fought as hard as I could, kicking and flailing my arms, knowing I only had a few minutes before water would fill my lungs. I was struggling to get to the surface when the hand let off my foot. I swam away, not looking back to see what happened. I broke the surface, gasping for air. Brady had my gun trained on Grayson, who was standing near the middle of the dock with his hands up. Holden surfaced while I was swimming back to the deck. He had his arms around a body—my attacker.

"Be careful! That's the killer!" I yelled.

"No, it's not! I need help," Holden called back. "It's my dad. Help me!"

I swam toward Holden and slid my arm underneath the weak body. The man was alive, but his head lulled to the side.

"I didn't know. I didn't know," Holden said.

"What happened?"

"I hit him really hard. I was going to let him drown, but the mask came off."

"Okay. He's going to be okay. Just keep his head above water and let's get him to shore."

Brady helped us pulled Chuck Timmons onto land. Holden performed CPR on his dad and Brady held me close, struggling to warm my shivering body.

The cops showed up a few minutes after we climbed back on the deck. Chuck was moaning by that time. Holden kept talking to him, keeping him conscious. The paramedics arrived soon after the police and Chuck Timmons was handcuffed and put in the back of an ambulance.

"You alright?" Brady asked, pulling me into a side hug and wrapping a towel around my shoulders.

I turned and made it into a full hug, throwing my arms around his neck.

"Thank you," I whispered in his ear.

"I'm so glad I was here. You okay?"

"Yeah. Chuck hit me in the back, but Grayson just talked to me. He clearly didn't seem to want all the violence. I don't think he was involved," I said pulling the towel tighter around my body. "Where did Holden come from?"

"He must have known Grayson was meeting with you. I hide in the trees when I saw headlights headed towards the parking lot. I confronted him when he parked. He didn't tell me anything, but we were arguing about why he just showed up when you screamed. We both ran towards your voice."

"Chuck Timmons. He wasn't on our radar at all."

"Did Grayson have a congregant kill his brother? Or did Chuck act alone?"

"I think we're going to have to wait and see," Brady said.

"I feel terrible for Holden." I said, letting go of Brady's neck and looking across the parking lot at Holden. He was leaning against his car. Darcy and his mother were there talking to him.

"Yeah, this was a total surprise to all of us."

"I guess Madalyn is off the hook now."

26

———————

Chuck Timmons had confessed to the murder of Nathan Broussard. It was a shock to the community because Chuck was a respected church-going man. He'd also worked with the Broussards for decades, so when Grayson gave him the opportunity to move up, he jumped at the chance. Unfortunately, the move to the corporate office required Chuck to help Grayson convince Nathan to accept a business deal with Lucian. After years of secret trips to the local casinos, Chuck had racked up a lot of debt. When Nathan refused to sign on the dotted line with Lucian, Chuck decided to get rid of the only person standing in the way of a huge payday.

Grayson Broussard was questioned but there wasn't enough evidence to prove he was involved in the murder plot. Krista was charged with filing a false police report, but only Chuck Timmons was charged in Nathan's murder. A few days after the news broke, Holden Timmons called to apologize for sneaking into my room several times and planting the doll under my bed.

"I thought Pastor Grayson had killed his brother. I know it

was wrong, but I wanted to protect him. He's my hero," Holden said.

I assured him all was forgiven and send him good wishes for his future.

As things resolved, Madalyn answered most of our questions.

Krista gave her twenty thousand dollars as a retainer. But by that time, she realized that Krista just wanted out of the marriage, and because of Nathan's position in life, she wanted to disappear. But Nathan wasn't ever violent with her and Madalyn was sure of that by New Year's Eve. She was going to give the money to Nathan during their meeting in the bayou.

A few days after Chuck Timmons confessed the three of us booked flights. Madalyn had decided that she needed vacation to make up for the crazy few weeks we'd spent in New Orleans.

"Next time I think you two should plan the vacation." Madalyn said before lifting her Margherita and taking a sip.

"You think we're ever going anywhere with you again?" Brady said.

We laughed and lifted our glasses for a toast. Brady and I were sipping glasses of merlot. The Jazz Garden at the airport was nice and while I wasn't looking forward to the single digit weather in Michigan, I was ready to go home.

"So Chuck Timmons did this all on his own?" Brady asked.

"That's what the police say. They've made a couple of bad arrests in this murder, so this time there was a lot of pressure for them to be as transparent as possible. Also, since Chuck Timmons confessed, we've got most of the story."

"Have you talked with Carson?" I asked.

Madalyn shook her head. "I thanked him in a message, but he didn't respond. That ship has sailed. He wanted me to throw you under the bus, like a sacrificial lamb. That doesn't align with who I am."

Madalyn was loyal and honest, even when it wasn't in her best interest. Carson lived in a different world.

"Why didn't you tell me about Nathan from the beginning?" I asked.

"Nathan cared about honor. He didn't want to disgrace his wife unless she really was falsely accusing him of being abusive. I worked up to asking him if he'd ever put his hands on her. He vehemently denied it and didn't believe that Krista had lied about him. I didn't want to sully her name unless I absolutely had to. It was for Nathan. He was a friend."

"What's going to happen to Krista now?" Brady asked.

"She's going back to Tennessee for a little while. Grayson said they're keeping the kids while Krista figures things out. Personally, I think they will end up with custody."

"Probably so. She seemed to want to be free of the life she was living. Sad story for the kids. They basically lose both parents. Can't imagine abandoning my family if I was a father to live a life alone."

"Some people change their minds after going so far down a path. Sometimes, I feel like I'm in that position, so I can't judge. I might not be a private investigator by this time next year."

Madalyn and Brady looked at me.

"Really?" Madalyn asked.

I shrugged my shoulders and said, "Stay tuned."

"It's always about love or money." Madalyn said.

"I never suspected Holden's father. We thought the son was the culprit." I said.

"But it all makes sense now. Chuck Timmons found himself deep in debt from a secret gambling habit. When Lucian Sevier presented the Broussards with the a business deal, Grayson told Chuck he would be named the supervisor of the new division. This would have meant a huge pay increase for Chuck." Madalyn said.

"Sad what people do for money." Brady added before we finished our drinks and prepared to head to our terminals.

"As always, it's been real, Sylvia." Brady said, giving me a hug before he headed off to his terminal. Madalyn was heading to Houston to see family, so I was flying back to Michigan alone.

"We were a pretty good team here."

"Yeah. Imagine if we were always a team," Brady said, winking at me as we broke our embrace.

"Simmer down, mister. We worked well together on this case. Who knows what will come our way...." I trailed off. A tall figure moved towards us. Abnormally fast. He was staring at me. An eerie smirk creased Lucian's face. My mouth dropped open.

"Are you okay?" Brady asked, shaking my arm. It took me a moment to snap out of the daze.

"Lucian! He's headed toward us moving fast... too fast?"

Brady looked around. "Where?"

"Right there," I said, pointing behind Brady.

Brady looked back at the people milling around, squinting his eyes. "Sylvia, I don't see anything that looks like Lucian."

"He's out there. I saw him."

Brady shook his head. "We really need to get you home. I hope you can sleep on the flight."

Brady walked me as far as he could, gave me a big hug and made me promise to call him when I got home.

"A text. Okay?"

Brady smiled and shook his head.

"I guess I have to take what I can get."

I was able to doze on the flight, but something kept waking

me up. I got home late that evening and Martin was waiting to pick me up. I hadn't realize how exhausted I was until I got into the car. My body and my mind begged for more sleep. Martin drove and talked for the first few minutes of the ride, but I drifted off. Unfortunately, I kept seeing Lucian's eyes in my head and snapping out of my light slumber. Was I losing my mind?

Martin shook me when we got to my place.

"You're finally home. Clearly you need some sleep. I bet next time when I tell you to stay away from Madalyn, you're going to listen, right?"

Martin giggled.

"I think I will, but you've got to admit that for all the trouble she is, Madalyn is loyal and dependable. At the end of the day, she's got a good heart."

"Yeah, whatever. Just stay away from her. She's trouble."

I nodded. Martin smirked, knowing that if Madalyn called right by the minute and needed help, I'd do what I could. We said our goodbyes, and I headed inside.

I glanced at my phone and saw I had ten missed calls, all from the same number. Father Keegan had been calling me excessively over the past few days. I wasn't in the mood to talk with him, so I silenced the phone again, as I'd done over and over again over the past few days. But I needed to face my demons, even if some of them involved talking to my old friend and former priest. I made a mental note to call him first thing in the morning, sent Brady text, crawled onto the couch, and drifted off to sleep.

ALSO BY BRAYLEE PARKINSON

Sylvia Wilcox Mysteries

Who She Was

Displacement

Fracture

A Sylvia Wilcox Christmas

Road To Nowhere

Awakening

Deviance

Penitent (2023)